YOU PLAN THE S ☑ P9-DLZ-296

Ride with Napoleon to defeat the Turks . . .
Save Queen Elizabeth's jewels from being
stolen . . .
Try to keep Thomas à Becket from losing his
head . . .
Join Robin Hood and his merry band in
Sherwood Forest . . .

What happens in this book is up to you,
according to the choices you make, page by
page. You'll find over thirty possible endings,
from scary to serious to surprising. And it all
begins when your dad wants to mix business
with pleasure by taking the whole family to
England.

Ask for these Making Choices titles from Chariot Books

GENERAL K'S
VICTORY TOUR

Donna Fletcher Crow

Illustrated by Al Bohl

Chariot Books
DAVID C. COOK PUBLISHING CO.

for John and Elizabeth
and our special friends,
Sarah Elizabeth and Ann Victoria Rose

Chariot Books is an imprint of David C. Cook
Publishing Co.
David C. Cook Publishing Co., Elgin, Illinois 60120
David C. Cook Publishing Co., Weston, Ontario

GENERAL K'S VICTORY TOUR

First printing, 1987
Printed in the United States of America
91 90 89 88 87   5 4 3 2 1

Library of Congress Cataloging-in-Publication Data

Crow, Donna Flecher.
  General K's victory tour.

  (A Making choices book)
  Summary: The reader's decisions control a series
of adventures involving travel into the past,
including visits to Napoleon, Queen Elizabeth, and
other historic figures.
  1. Plot-your-own stories. [1. Space and time—
Fiction. 2. Plot-your-own stories] I. Bohl, Al, ill. II.
Title. III. Series.
[PZ7.C88533Ge 1987]   [Fic]   86-13413
ISBN 1-555-13034-8

CAUTION!

This is not a normal book! If you read it straight through, it won't make sense.

Instead, you must start at page 1 and then turn to the pages where your choices lead you. One moment you're admiring the Tower of London, and the next moment you find yourself transported back in time to the bloody fields of the Megiddo Valley in Palestine. Studying battle strategy with General K turns out to be more exciting and dangerous than you thought.

If you want to read this book, you must choose to
Turn to page 1.

"England?! for the whole summer?" Forgetting you're at the dinner table, you fling out your arm and send your glass of milk flying.

Your mom sighs and hands you a rag. "That was the idea, but you'll need to develop some proper manners first. I don't want everyone thinking American children are uncivilized."

While you mop up under your soggy place mat, your dad continues. "As I was saying, I have a business conference to attend in London. You kids are old enough to get a lot out of the trip, so we thought we'd make a family vacation of it."

You jab your finger in the direction of your nine-year-old sister, Elizabeth. "Lizard, too?"

"How many times have I told you *not* to call your sister that terrible name?" Your mom frowns at you. Before you can answer, she goes on. "I'll pick you up after school tomorrow, and we'll get your passport pictures taken."

But your mind is on what you'll tell your friends. Just wait till Chris hears about this! Of course, after all the adventures the two of you have had flying Professor Q's time machine around the Bible lands, even England might get a little dull. Maybe the Prof could reprogram AL's cartograph. . . .

"Huh?" You suddenly realize your dad is speaking to you.

"I said, so we think we can be ready to go the week after school is out. Okay?"

Turn to page 2.

Three weeks later, a big black taxi drives you from Heathrow Airport along the Thames River, right past the Houses of Parliament. You think normal means of travel might have some advantages.

You don't even bother unpacking your suitcase when you get to your hotel. "Well, let's go. I want to go see stuff!"

"I want to take a nap," your mom says, dropping into a chair. "Don't you feel jet lagged?"

You grin at her in a superior way—if she'd flown around in AL the way you have. . . .

Your dad flops down beside her. "We could get a nanny to show the kids around."

You outgrew Mary Poppins years ago, but it beats sitting around a hotel room while your folks sleep. So you pick up the London telephone directory and look under "baby-sitting."

When the nanny arrives, you decide she might not be such a bad idea. She's young and attractive and has a nice smile.

"Hi, I'm Heather," she says. "What do you want to do? We could stay around London or take a train out into the country."

Choices: You want to visit a London site (turn to page 26).
You choose to go someplace in the English countryside (turn to page 4).

"Why do you want to see Deborah?" you ask.

"Because a woman military leader is unique in any age, but especially in her time. She had to make a battle plan against mighty King Jabin, who had kept Israel in subjection for twenty years with his force of 900 iron chariots. Now *that's* the kind of strategy NATO could put to use."

"How?" you ask. "Are the Russians building iron chariots?"

The general gives you a quelling look, but explains, "If we can be sure of our superior strategy, we can more freely go ahead with arms limitations talks."

"Wow! You mean something we're doing now might save the world from the bomb?" Chris asks.

"I certainly hope so," General K says.

But you are quiet. There's something the general has overlooked. You're not sure whether you should mention it to him or not.

Choices: You argue with General K (turn to page 52).

You go along with Chris and the general (turn to page 86).

"Come on," Heather says. "We'll take the tube." You follow her to the sign of a big red circle with a red bar running straight across it that says "Underground." She buys your tickets and leads the way to the escalator.

You do down. Way down. Then you go down again. "Hey, I didn't choose *China*," you say.

Heather grins and takes you to another down escalator. At the landing of this one are a fellow playing a harmonica and a girl tap dancing. You watch them for a minute and then toss a shilling, which Heather says is the same as an American nickel, into the guy's hat.

Just then you hear a loud rumbling sound. Heather grabs you and pulls you to the electric train. She and Elizabeth get seats, but you stand up, holding tight to a strap as the train roars out of the station.

Next to you is a man wearing a three-piece suit and a bowler hat, carrying a briefcase and umbrella. The girl sitting next to Elizabeth has bright pink hair and is wearing about a thousand chain necklaces. It takes all kinds. . . .

After several stops you arrive at Paddington Station. Elizabeth dashes ahead, crying, "Oh, I hope Paddington Bear is here!"

You start to run after her when two men walk by carrying black swords and numchucks. One wears a jacket that says "Edwinstowe School of Ninjutsu."

Choices: You chase Elizabeth (turn to page 81).
You leave Elizabeth to Heather and follow the Ninjas (turn to page 54).

You wait three days and in that time eat four small oatcakes, a piece of cheese, and six dates. You're about to give up when news comes— King Richard the Lionheart has arrived.

You run to the wharf to see him disembark. It's easy to pick him out. A head taller than anyone else, he is a handsome, muscular man with red gold hair.

"He has a high soul and strong heart," someone near you says.

"Yes," another replies, "his courage is dauntless."

Richard strides across the gangplank, the sun glinting off his chain mail, his white surcoat shining, and the cross emblazoned on his chest a glowing red. When he is almost in front of you, he raises his great two-hand sword, just like the one you saw in the Tower. He brandishes it over his head in a salute to his troops . . . and collapses in a heap at your feet.

"King Richard has been very sick on the trip!" a servant cries, rushing forward. "We had storms, fever, and seasickness."

Richard is moaning at your feet. You kneel and hold his head in your lap, your heart sinking with disappointment. How can you win a war with a sick leader and starving troops?

Choices: You stay with Richard (turn to page 32).

You look around for General K (turn to page 74).

With a rustle of leaves, Robin Hood jumps to the ground near you. "Hello, my friends. Welcome to Sherwood Forest. You have had the honor of observing His Majesty at the hunt."

"Yes, sir. But it is more of an honor to meet the famous Robin Hood."

He throws his head back and laughs at your compliment; then he sweeps his hat off and bows. "And how may I serve so gallant tongued a friend?"

"It is King Richard you can serve, if you choose," you say.

"God save King Richard."

"He'll have to. John is trying to take over the throne."

"Just as I suspected," Robin says. "Come, let's join my men and hold counsel."

You follow him through the woods to a clearing on the far side of a secluded thicket, and there are all of Robin Hood's band of merry men: Little John, Friar Tuck, Will Scarlet, Allen-a-Dale. You feel you know them, you've read of them so often.

Little John fills big wooden plates with tasty stew. While you sit around eating, everyone shares his idea of what should be done about Prince John.

Choices: You think John should be stopped by action (turn to page 48).
You think John should be stopped by diplomacy (turn to page 37).

The massive stone cathedral is as cold inside as the winter day outside. At first you think you're the only ones there; then you hear some monks chanting vespers at the far end of the great chancel. Staying behind the huge stone pillars that line the room like a primeval forest, you slip forward. The gloomy cavern is lit by dozens of flickering candles, and the monks' chant echoes on the stones.

Suddenly a tall man wearing bishop's robes and a miter comes through a side door carrying a cross.

"No, no, Lord Thomas, I beg you," one of the monks cries. "It is the king's men!"

"Unbar the door! Let anyone who wishes come into the house of God. And God's will be done."

Two monks remove the heavy wooden bar from the door they locked soon after you entered. The four angry knights burst into the church. The monks gather around as you move closer.

"Where is Thomas à Becket, traitor to the king and realm?" a knight yells. There is no answer.

"Where is the archbishop?"

Thomas answers, "I am here—no traitor, but a priest."

The Knight of the Bear rattles his sword on the stone floor. "Do you realize you owe everything to the king?"

"Certainly not," Thomas answers. "We must

render to the king the things that are the king's, and to God the things that are God's."

"Then you shall die!" The knight raises his sword.

Choices: You watch quietly (turn to page 76). You try to stop the murder (turn to page 71).

You follow Deborah and Barak and their ten thousand, ragged guerrilla fighters up the side of Mount Tabor and turn to look back across the barren, rocky valley beneath dark, brooding clouds. Then you wish you hadn't looked. "General, how many men does Sisera have?"

General K pulls out the field glasses he refused to leave in AL and scans the valley. "Three hundred thousand infantry, ten thousand cavalry, and no fewer than three thousand chariots, I should say."

You gulp. But Deborah looks undaunted, standing on top of the hill with her arms held out, her white robe billowing in the wind beneath her mantle. "Have faith—for this is the day the Lord will deliver us!" she cries. You certainly hope so.

Deborah gives the signal, and Barak charges down the mountain at the head of his troops as lightning flashes above him and thunder shakes the mountain. In the excitement, you rush forward yelling with the soldiers, waving your arms as if you were carrying a sword.

All at once a bolt of lightning strikes so close you fall back. The clouds burst open, sending torrents of rain streaming on the heavily armored Canaanite troops and turning the entire valley into a sea of mud.

Turn to page 63.

While you hesitate, she enters the tent and then returns immediately with a pottery bowl. "Quickly. He has asked for water, but I shall serve him milk. There—" she points. "Go milk the goat for me. Hurry, it is important."

You've never milked a goat—or anything else—before. "Baaa, nice billy," you say, walking forward with your hand held out.

The goat looks up from the clump of grass she's munching and takes a step backward.

"Halt!" the general barks. The goat stops.

General K makes a kind of halter out of his field glasses strap and secures the goat. "Proceed."

Making a face at Chris, you give him the bowl to hold under the goat. You squat down beside it. "Yuck! These things smell bad." But you can't hold your nose because you need both hands to squeeze the milk out. At first nothing comes. Then a small white trickle squirts on the ground. You adjust your aim, and this time you squirt yourself. Chris laughs while you wipe the warm, sticky liquid off your eyes, but he doesn't laugh when the next squirt gets him in the ear.

Then you wonder if it's part of God's plan for Sisera to drink milk—if so, you'd better concentrate on this business.

Finally you have a bowl of warm, rich milk for Jael. She smiles as she takes it from you. "Now, help me stand guard. Sisera wishes to sleep. If anyone comes, say there is nobody here."

Turn to page 18.

You enter Sherwood Forest in search of Prince John. Massive trees grow thick, but the sun filters down between the leaves, allowing green grass and underbrush to cover the ground.

You think you could wander for days and find no one, but suddenly a deer bounds across the path right in front of you, pursued by yapping hounds. A hunting horn sounds through the air, followed by the crash of horses.

You run fast enough to glimpse the deer breaking through into a meadow. Then the hunters are on her—and at the center of the party is a bearded young man wearing a gold coronet over his hood. When an archer addresses him as Your Majesty, you know it's Prince John.

John shoots an arrow that kills the deer,

shouting, "And may a Saracen arrow do the same to my brother Richard!"

"The throne shall be yours, Sire," a lackey says.

"Should we go to him now?" you ask Chris.

Before Chris can answer, you hear a chuckle above you. You look up and see a man in a green hat with his bow slung over his shoulder and the carcasses of two deer hanging high in the tree Prince John just rode under. Such a daring poacher in the King's hunting preserve could only be Robin Hood!

Choices: You follow Prince John (turn to page 140).

You stay with Robin Hood (turn to page 7).

You stuff your pockets with gold, put handfuls of jewels under your hat, and take off your cloak to make a pack to fill with treasure. It's *very* heavy, and the clinking and clanking sound loud in the night air as you steal to the mouth of the cave.

It's still pitch black, and you don't spot any guards, so you start forward. Going down is lots harder than going up was—especially since you're weighted with about 200 pounds of gold—but you're very cautious.

Not cautious enough, though. Your cloak catches on a sharp rock and rips. You know you're leaving a trail of gold coins, but clinging to the edge of the dirt cliff, you don't see any way to repair your cape. At least your load's getting lighter.

Then a loose rock under your foot sends you rolling. Your hat falls off, and the jewels scatter. "Oh, well, they were giving me a headache anyway," you mutter.

By the time you get to the foot of the cliff, you have less than half the booty you started out with. Should you give it to Robin Hood to give to the poor? take it back home with you? give it to K for national defense? to your church for missions? or maybe buy that new three-wheeler and fancy stereo and computer?

For the first time you begin to see what people mean when they say being rich has its problems, too.

THE END

Leaving Elizabeth and Heather with General K, you and Chris wait until dark and slip down the side of the valley into the Turkish camp. There are thousands of tents; it's impossible to tell which one is the commander's.

You try to keep to the shadows, but there is a bare patch of ground you must cross to get to the center of the camp. You are halfway across when you see a flickering torch. A guard shouts, "Halt!"

Choices: You halt (turn to page 38).
You run (turn to page 98).

You get back to Paddington just in time to jump on the train with Heather and Elizabeth.

"We're going to Sherwood Forest! I'm going to see Robin Hood!" Elizabeth says.

There is a little country fair on the edge of the forest. Elizabeth and Heather stop to buy some cotton candy, but you keep walking up the trail.

Then you hear soneone calling your name . . .

Turn to page 55.

As soon as it's dark you walk quietly to the castle hill, towering hundreds of feet above everything else. Around the far side of the hill you search the dirt cliff for the caves.

You wish it weren't so dark, but if the moon were bright you might be seen. Is that an opening? You hurry forward, but it's just a dark boulder in the dirt. You are working your way up the side of the hill when some loose dirt under your feet slips, and you start to fall. You clutch at the nearest rock, and finally stop yourself by digging your heels into the soft ground.

You look back from where you fell and then you see it—the rock was hiding the entrance to a cave. You scramble back up the hill. Inside the cave, no one can see you, so you light a candle. You have to crawl, but the cave does turn into a tunnel. With mounting excitement you crawl faster and faster, wondering how long it'll take you to get inside the castle.

"Ouch!" you yell and rub your head. You've run into the end of the tunnel. You start to crawl back out when you yell, "Ouch!" again. You've hit your foot on something sharp. Setting your candle on a rock, you dig it out—a heavy casket buried inside the cave. You keep digging. There are three more.

You hit the lock off with a rock. Gold and jewels.

Choices: You decide to send it to Richard (turn to page 80).

You want to keep it (turn to page 14).

You haven't stood very long until you hear snoring in the tent and see Jael slip inside. You wonder why she's carrying a long, pointed tent peg with her.

A little while later Barak arrives, looking for Sisera.

"Come, and I will show you the man for whom you are looking," Jael says.

There is the Canaanite general on the floor of the tent, the wooden spike driven through his head. You're surprised to see how shaken General K looks.

"Haven't you seen worse things than that in battles?" you ask.

"Certainly. But don't you see—the prophecy. This morning we heard Deborah tell Barak that God would deliver Sisera into the hands of a woman. I thought she meant herself, and when Sisera escaped I thought she—or God—was wrong."

"Have to rethink it now, huh?" you say.

The general is too busy thinking to answer you.

THE END

You charge forward, swinging your sword from side to side, as much to deflect the blows of others as to wound anyone. Then you see a Saracen riding straight for you. You grip your reins and hold your sword ready—three strides and you'll clash—

But you never make three strides. Your horse puts his foot in a rabbit hole and pitches forward, throwing you over his neck and flinging your sword and shield into the desert sands.

You lie there, stunned, and then roll over quickly as the sharp hooves of a horse gallop right over you.

"Oooo!" You put your hand to your head, and then wish you hadn't when you see the blood on it.

"Well, you're alive," Chris says. "But I don't know how we're going to explain that head to your nanny."

"Maybe we can say a broadsword from the Tower fell on it—that wouldn't exactly be a lie." General Kempthorne and Chris laugh, but you don't think it's very funny.

THE END

General K and Chris are waiting for you outside the tent.

"Richard ordered breaching the walls. Sir Guy is leading the attack on the north tower." You point.

"Aha, precisely what I should do." General K follows the knight, and you follow the general.

The Crusaders have a huge siege tower. The first story is built of wood, the second of lead, the third of iron, and the fourth of bronze. It stands taller than the ramparts of Acre, but has been kept back out of range. Now, under Richard's order, it is pulled into placed with long ropes.

"Ought to cover that thing with rawhides so it won't burn—Greek fire's a nasty thing," General K mutters.

An archer standing near laughs. "Lead, iron, and bronze won't burn."

Then Sir Guy orders you into the tower. General K starts to argue that he doesn't take orders, he gives them; then he turns to command you, "Forward!"

Turn to page 150.
Turn to page 150.

The next morning Robin Hood's spies report that the nobles are meeting in Nottingham.

"Great. But how do we get in?" Chris asks.

You think for awhile. "You got any fancy clothes in that stuff you've stolen, Robin?" you ask.

He sure does. The general dresses as a nobleman and Chris as a page boy. You put on a monk's robe.

General K plays the part perfectly as he swaggers into the meeting. "The duke of Kempthorne demands to know why he hasn't been advised of this meeting!" he roars at the earls. He is hastily offered a seat and profuse apologies.

"Now, what I want to know is what you plan to do about this pip-squeak Prince John. We can't sit back and let him take over King Richard's throne. Richard will have all our heads off when he returns."

Rubbing his neck, the Earl of Salisbury quickly agrees. "What do you suggest?"

"My friend, er—Brother AL here, has a suggestion." K points to you.

You pull the prepared document from the folds of your robe. "Prince John must be made to sign this, swearing his allegiance to Richard. Then let John know you intend to enforce it."

The Earl of Pembroke strides toward you, frowning.

Turn to page 24.

It's a long, tiring, way back across the desert to the spot where you left AL, but all the way you have visions of green, green England and your comfortable hotel to keep you slogging through the sand.

You quickly locate the two scrubby olive trees you parked AL between. General Kempthorne starts barking orders at you about where he wants to go and when, but you can't think of anything but getting back to modern conveniences.

At first you think Chris's groans are his response to K's demand; then you realize it's something worse. Much, much worse.

"Well, I told you Prof Q said the chip could slip—I just didn't think it would really happen . . . ."

"So what do you suggest now?" Your voice is cold with anger.

"Well, I did bring some computer games. We don't need a working cartograph chip for that. Look, I've got ZORK and Ms. Pac-Man and Star Raiders and Frogger and—"

It's a good thing General K is between the two of you, or there would be murder. You're stuck in the middle of a sea of barren sand, and Chris wants you to play Ms. Pac-Man.

THE END

Giant, shadowy figures seem to loom from the smoke that fills every corner of the dim room. The witch, draped in green and purple robes, is bending over the flames, her arms upraised. Saul's servants don't even see you as they carry their unconscious king out.

Chris nudges you and moves forward. You follow, trying to think of something to ask the witch. What dead person do you want to talk to?

"This is dumb. We don't need a witch—we've got AL," you whisper to Chris as you approach the fire.

The witch turns to you, dark shadows writhing across her sharp features.

Suddenly the tent is filled with hysterical shrieks. The smoke churns and billows with a form running through it. Your eyes are burning and watery, but you can see it's no ghostly spirit nor the Witch of Endor raising the alarm—it's your sister.

"I want out! I hate witches! Help!" Elizabeth tears out of the tent and down toward the valley.

You run after her, clear to the camp of the Israelites. And that's where you are a few hours later when the Philistines attack, and Saul and his sons and all his army are killed.

THE END

The Earl rips the paper from your hand and reads it aloud. At the end he turns so fast he almost knocks you over with his powerful fist. He grabs your hand and shakes it. "Well done, Brother AL. Let's go to the Prince. Aye, and he'll sign or answer to me." He drags you with him as he strides from the room, not stopping for breath until he is standing before Prince John in his royal chamber.

The cowardly John looks at the mighty nobles standing around him. "What can I do for you, gentlemen?"

It takes him less than five minutes to sign the document with a quill pen, drop a pool of melted wax below his signature, and press his signet ring into it.

"And now," the Earl of Pembroke says, "We shall seal this occasion with prayer. Brother AL will lead us."

You gulp. All you can think of is, "Now I lay me down to sleep." You see the others crossing themselves, so you do, too, and then fold your hands. Just in time you remember that they prayed in Latin in those days. Silently praying a *real* prayer that no one in the room knows real Latin, you begin, "Ourya Atherfay, oohay arya inya evanhay, ivgay usya isthay. . . ."

THE END

"Now be careful when you cross the streets here. We drive on the other side of the street, and that means you'll have to look in the 'wrong' direction for traffic." Heather points to the warning painted on the street with an arrow, LOOK RIGHT.

Sure enough, Elizabeth looks left, doesn't see any traffic, and starts across right in front of a car.

Heather screams.

You jump off the curb, grab Elizabeth, and fall backwards together. The car rushes by so close you can feel the swish of air.

"Oh, well done!" Heather pulls you both to your feet and wipes you off. "How about an ice cream?" she says quickly, as Elizabeth looks ready to burst into tears.

She takes you to the ice-cream truck on a corner in Hyde Park. Elizabeth orders a cherry ice in the shape of a teddy bear. You're so glad she's all right, you don't even think it's dumb, but you're still shaking too much inside to eat.

"When do we get to ride on a double-decker bus?" you ask, seeing one of the big red vehicles rush by.

"As soon as you decide where you want to go. Do you want to do the Tower of London first or the Houses of Parliament?"

Choices: You vote for the Tower of London (turn to page 93).
You want to see the Houses of Parliament (turn to page 107).

Following Robin's directions, you head into the forest. But it's not as simple as he made it sound. "He said to turn right at the Major Oak, but which one is that? They all look huge to me," Chris says.

"Our teacher told us about that when we read Robin Hood," you say. "It's thirty feet around and hollow, so twelve of Robin Hood's men can hide in it. But I don't see it anywhere."

"There's some men!" Elizabeth starts running between the trees. "Little John! Friar Tuck!"

"Come here, pretty maiden." One of them holds his hand out to her. "You think we be Robin Hood's men, do ye?"

Another one laughs. "We'll treat you better than those outlaws would. Come along, missy, I'll find you a sweet."

"How much do you reckon her folks'll pay to get her back?" another one says, as they disappear into the woods with Elizabeth.

They are kidnapping your sister!

Choices: You follow them (turn to page 75).
You seek Robin's men to help you (turn to page 134).

No need to change the cartograph. You just set AL's chronograph for the end of the 12th century and slip into one of the costumes Prof Q sent along.

You get out beside a dirt road. Tulips and daffodils are blooming in the soft green grass, and young birds sing in the trees. Elizabeth claps her hands and does a little dance. A man with a red beard, wearing a green cap, comes riding out of the woods just in time to see her.

"It's May, it's May, the merry month of May . . ." he sings in a jolly voice.

"Robin Hood?" you ask.

"You don't be the sheriff's spies, do ye?" he says with a laugh.

But before you can answer, an old woman hobbles toward you, leaning heavily on a stick. "Oh, woe, woe," she cries.

"What's this?" Robin asks. "What news have you, old mother?"

"There's three squires in Nottinghamtown today is condemned to die!" she sobs. "My sons, they be."

"Condemned to die! Then they must be dangerous criminals! What have they done?" Robin Hood asks.

"Nay, sir, nay. Not dangerous they be. It's for slaying of the king's fallow deer."

"They're gonna hang men for shooting a *deer*?" you ask.

Robin Hood nods. "Yes, indeed. And they may hang me for attempting a rescue. But try I must. You may wait in the forest with my men. Tell Little John what I go to do."

Choices: You say, "I'll be glad to take your message" (turn to page 27).
You say, "I'd rather accompany you, sir" (turn to page 36).

With both hands in front of you, you blast out the door and barrel down the corridor. You're really racing by the time you reach the main door and shoot out onto the sidewalk. If you can make it across the street to the park, maybe you can hide in the bushes.

You are halfway across the street when you run smack into a bobby directing traffic.

"And what's all the 'urry about, my friend?" he asks, holding your arm.

"I, er—I'm late for tea." You think your answer is brilliant.

But your confidence dissolves when the police officer says, "Tea, is it now? At eleven o'clock in the morning? And since when did Americans 'ave tea time?"

"Well, er—" you stammer.

"I think we'd better just go for a little walk. Seems as if His Right Honourableness your ambassador might want to 'ear why you come out of that building at a speed to break all records."

He hauls you back the way you just came and takes you to a private room. But you aren't private long. Two big American Marines march in the door.

Turn to page 95.

You walk out into the desert until a thin red line of sunrise shows over the hill country to the east. With the first rays of sun, you begin hearing the haunting, lonesome calls of desert birds.

Their melancholy sound suits your mood perfectly. You can't believe Chris could be gone. You can't figure out how to cope with it. Another bird calls closer to you.

Well, you'll have to go back. Maybe the best thing would be to telegraph Prof Q from London. Or ask the general if the Pentagon could break it to Chris's folks. . . .

A shrill whistle pierces the air close to you. You jerk your head up. That wasn't a bird. You turn and start to run, but it's too late. A marauding band of Bedouins have you surrounded.

As you are hauled off by your captors, your only cheerful thought is that at least you won't have to tell Chris's folks.

But who will tell yours?

THE END

Richard is borne to his tent in a litter. Soon the supplies he brought are unloaded, and everyone is eating. This is the first real food some of the men have had for weeks, and there is great celebration in camp.

But inside Richard's tent, the mood is somber. The fevered King refuses the dried biscuits and warm wine he is offered, and the camp physician wrings his hands. "If only he had something cool in this heat. If only . . ."

His pacing is interrupted by a man with dark skin, wearing a red and purple turban and carrying a basket. The Crusaders in the tent draw their swords, but the man sets his basket down and bows in each direction. "His Highness, the exalted servant of Allah, Sultan Saladin, sends greetings. He is disturbed to hear that His English Highness is ill. Lord Saladin sends fresh fruit from Jezreel and snow from the mountains. Please accept his gift."

The Saracen bows his way out of the tent. The knights put up their swords and the physician rushes to the basket. The fruit, packed in crystal white snow, looks like a casket of red, green, and gold jewels. It is undoubtedly sweet and juicy, and could be life giving for Richard.

But can Saladin be trusted? The physician looks at you. Will you taste it?

Choices: You say, "Please pass the peaches" (turn to page 129)
You say, "I've got an appointment with a general" (turn to page 118).

You have certainly chosen the army with might on its side. You follow along beside the powerful Canaanite charioteers and see why they held military supremacy in their part of the world for so long. Heavily armored, the mighty war machines move forward across the plain, their sturdy war-horses unflinching as lightning flashes around them and thunder rolls across the sky.

A foot soldier beside you gives a scathing laugh. "Look at Barak's men—like ants on the mountainside. What do they think they can do against the troops of King Jabin?"

"And look!" Another soldier points up the mountainside. "They have a woman with them! Wouldn't go to war without their mother!" Raucous laughter fills the ranks.

But the merriment is drowned in a clap of thunder that shakes the ground under you. Then the sky opens in a torrent of rain that halts even the charioteers' mighty chargers. Within minutes the dusty desert floor is turned into a muddy riverbed. The heavy Canaanite chariots sink up to their wheel shafts and sit useless as beached boats.

"To the river!" the soldier next to you cries. With the others you retreat toward the Kishon

River, only to find that it is already overflowing its banks. The Canaanites who try to swim sink under the weight of their heavy armor. And even some of you who aren't wearing armor find the deluge too much to fight against. . . .

THE END

"Would you, indeed? Well, come on then." Robin starts into town. Soon you meet an old man walking along the road. "My good fellow," Robin Hood calls. "Would you like a new suit? Change clothes with me!"

Robin Hood tosses the man his sturdy cloak and puts on the beggar's garment made of patched flour sacks. The breeches, hose and shoes are just as ragged, but the disguise works. A mile down the road you meet the sheriff.

"Greetings, bold Sheriff," Robin hails him. "What will you give a poor old man to be your hangman today?"

"I see you need new clothes. I'll give you a suit and thirteen pence for three hangings."

"Done!" Robin says. "I've a horn in my pocket; I'll blow for my mates to help build your gallows." He jumps on a rock and blows a loud blast which brings his men running to town.

The gallows is built in a green field, and the sheriff brings out the prisoners. Then Robin gives another blast on his horn. Fifty men ride from the woods, pull the condemned men up onto horses, and ride off.

"Next time you try to hang my men, Sheriff, you'll be the one to swing!" Robin shouts as he disappears into the woods.

You are left alone with the sheriff. "Er—we were just watching, Mr. Sheriff, sir. I never saw those guys before in my life." You back up, grab Elizabeth's hand, and run for the woods.

THE END

"We'll need the help of the nobles who are still loyal to Richard," Little John says. "The Earl of Pembroke, the Earl of Essex, the Earl of Salisbury. If they join us, Prince John will have to see reason."

Robin laughs, "That's the one good thing about having a weak ruler—you can force him to your viewpoint."

"Until the next person forces him the other way," Friar Tuck says.

"That's why we *must* have the prince's signature and seal." Robin holds out a long sheet of parchment on which Friar Tuck has written the rules you want the prince to agree to.

"Do you think it will work?" you ask General K.

"It should," he says with a nod. "King John was later forced into signing the Magna Carta, which is the charter of Englishmen's individual rights—and the beginning of your American Bill of Rights."

"Great!" You jump up. "Let's go!"

"First we must persuade the nobles. As outlaws we have certain disadvantages in that area. That is why you must undertake the task." Robin Hood looks at you.

Choices: You think the nobles can be persuaded with arguments (turn to page 21).
You think you'll need something stronger than words (turn to page 42).

You have time for only a whispered word to Chris before the guard is upon you, but out of the corner of your eye you see your friend get away unseen. You've never been more thankful for Prof Q's instant language translator than when the Turkish guard starts shouting at you in his native tongue. He goes on and on, finally stopping with, "What are you doing here?"

"Well, you see, there was this guy named Aladdin, and his uncle took him to a cave and told him to lift up the stone and take the treasure in it. . . ." You put all your energy into holding the guard's interest. "And Aladdin found this magic lamp and when he rubbed it, a huge genie appeared . . ."

Unfortunately, that is too much for even your not-too-bright guard to believe. He moves toward you threateningly. "That is enough! You are a spy for the French! You have come from Napoleon." His features look evil and mean in the light of the torch. He reaches out toward you, pulls the scimitar out of his belt, and prepares to swing.

You feel the swirl of sand you've been waiting for. "Back to the future," you say, and step into AL.

THE END

You sit down under a palm tree. There are a few stars and a slim crescent moon in the sky. You hear sounds of the river flowing a few yards away. At last the peace of it gets to you, and you're calm enough to pray.

But what can you say? It's too late to pray for Chris. You need help getting through this, but it seems selfish to pray for yourself when Chris . . . You shudder in spite of the warmth of the evening.

When you bow your head, all you're able to say is, "Help. Please help."

But that's enough. You've no more than said the words, when you know what to do!"

"General K! General! Come on, let's go!" You practically drag the general into AL.

You're shaking so you can hardly set the instruments, but the general sees what you're doing. "Why, yes, of course! I should have thought of that!"

A moment later you set the last dial and hold your breath.

"Well, what are you waiting for? Let's go join Richard," Chris says beside you.

He gets the strangest look on his face when you grab him and start crying. "It worked! I set it back to yesterday, and you're all right!"

"Sure, I'm fine. What's the big deal?"

"Nothing. Nothing at all. Just . . . a bad dream I had," you say. Only you and the general and God know that it wasn't.

THE END

King Philip of France is directing the troops in building mangonels—catapults that sling stones great distances from a spoon-shaped bar, using the force of twisted ropes. The one you're working on is called God's Own Sling.

You are directed to lash the foot of the spoon-shaped bar to the crossbeam. "Get that rope tight—tighter," a knight barks at you. "That's what gives the spring to the sling."

You pull on the ropes until your hands blister. Then the order comes to push the machine into place. For the next few days you help to fling enormous stones against the city wall or over the wall to kill warriors inside. All the time a rain of arrows falls around you. But it's not fear of the arrows that makes you stop—it's the order to fling the body of a dead cow over the walls, where it will rot and cause disease.

The Crusades were supposed to be holy wars, fought to keep the land of Christ's birth under Christian rule. All the Crusaders take a vow in the name of God and wear a cross; even your catapult is named God's Own—but *is* this what God wants?

Your thoughts are interrupted as victory cries announce that at last the Crusaders have broken into Acre. You join in the celebration, but the next morning you're still wondering.

Choices: You march to Jerusalem with King Richard (turn to page 50).
You return home with King Philip of France (turn to page 114).

The general picks up the battle-ax a Crusader left sticking in the mud. With one smooth swing, he takes the top off the urn.

"It's a scroll or something." You plunge your hand into it.

"Careful, don't get it wet," Chris says.

"Feels like parchment. I don't think water will hurt that."

"But what if it crumbles? That may have been there since Bible times."

"Yeah," you say with a laugh, "but Bible times aren't so long ago as they used to be."

Chris and the general gather around, and you unroll the scroll.

Turn to page 69.

"We'll give each noble a bag of gold," you say. "Got any lying around, Robin?"

"Gave the last we had to a starving widow. But my spies report a delivery from the royal treasury on its way to the castle at dawn."

"Hmm. Maybe the delivery men will be hungry." You send Little John off to get some things, while you help Friar Tuck bake bread.

Next morning you and Chris start down the road dressed as peasant girls carrying trays of bread; Robin Hood's men wait in the woods.

A coach rumbles around the corner. Pretending it hit you, you fling your rolls in every direction. The horses rear and kick. The driver yells at Chris to get you out of the road. Chris thrusts his tray of goodies to the driver to hold while he helps you.

In the confusion, Robin Hood's men are supposed to come take the gold. But you hadn't figured on the sheriff riding guard behind.

"You got a permit to sell those?" a guard growls.

"We aren't selling them, we're giving them," Chris answers, and then gasps because he forgot to change his voice.

"You don't sound like no baker's daughter," the sheriff pulls the scarf off Chris's head. "This looks like one of Robin Hood's dumb plots."

"It's not! I thought of it myself!" you yell, but you realize that won't help you much as you are dragged off to the Nottingham jail.

THE END

Napoleon and a few of his closest officers ride up into the hills of Galilee to the village of Nazareth. The soldiers, who include General K in their group, talk about the strategy of the victorious battle. You look around the little village, remembering that it was the boyhood home of Jesus—these same hills, the same rocks, must have been here when he was a boy.

The buildings are square and snow white, just as you'd imagined them, framed by dark green, spear-shaped cypress trees. You ride down the Street of Carpenters, where in every arched doorway you see a man at work sawing wood, or hammering, or using a plane and chisel.

It's all so peaceful and quiet after the exhilaration and noise of the battle. Children run down the street chasing a puppy, laughing. You remember the screams of the men dying on the battlefield and the looters stripping their gold and jewels from them.

Napoleon enters a large house. You can smell food cooking; it makes your mouth water, but you tell Heather and the others to go on in. You want to sit in the evening shade of a cypress tree and think.

You think about the battle and about the man who lived here so long ago who said, "Peace I leave with you, my peace I give unto you; not as the world giveth, give I unto you." Is that the wisdom that the Bible says is more valuable than gold and rubies?

THE END

"Okay, okay. We'll go for a walk." But you can't find your sneakers, and Elizabeth is impatient. "Okay, go on out—but stay close. I'll catch up in a minute." You dig under your cot, but your shoes aren't there.

Ten minutes later, when you go out in Chris's tennis shoes, Elizabeth is nowhere in sight. This army is going to attack the enemy in an hour and a half, and you can't find your sister. "Elizabeth! Lizard! Liz!"

You follow the smell of coffee to the mess hall where the men are finishing breakfast, but there's no little girl in a pink jogging suit. "Lizard!" you yell, but in the commotion of preparing for battle no one even looks at you.

You think she might have gone looking for General K, so you head for the command post. Inside the small building, all is quiet, intense activity as each person focuses on his task with life-or-death concentration. And in the center of it all is your sister, perched on a high stool by General Allenby's desk, licking a big red lollipop.

"Elizabeth! What do you think you're doing bothering General Allenby at a time like this? Don't you know he's preparing for battle?" you scold.

Allenby shakes his head. "Let her stay. She's a reminder of what we're fighting to keep the world free for. Besides—" the general's voice catches and he swallows. "I had a child once. He was killed in action last year in France." He turns abruptly back to his charts.

You don't know what to do, but Elizabeth does. She jumps off her stool and gives Sir Edmund Allenby a lollipop-sticky kiss on the cheek.

THE END

"Who wants witches and ghosts when it isn't even Halloween?" you say, as you set AL to take you back to Allenby. You arrive in time for the signing of the armistice with Turkey.

General Kempthorne is ecstatic. "Captured 75,000 prisoners, took 360 guns, destroyed all the enemies' transport. And his own casualties are minimal. This is a man who can help keep the free world free!"

"But, sir, he already has. I mean, he did his thing."

"Yes, yes. But 'Old soldiers never die' and all that. We *must* take him back."

"Take him back! He'd be 125 years old! Besides, we don't have cavalries anymore—this was the last, remember?"

General K looks at you as if *you're* the one who's gone bonkers. "Not the man—his spirit!"

Spirit? You think of the shadowy spirit of the prophet Samuel you saw in the witch's tent last night. This is getting worse and worse. "Sir, I really don't think—"

"I've watched him at work for days—inspiring trust and confidence in his men. I've seen his absolute grasp of the facts and most of all, his moral courage and integrity. If I can take a vision for these things back, we'll be able to—how is it you Americans say it? To 'Secure the blessings of liberty to our children and our children's children.' "

THE END

Your sister and Heather are waiting for you where you left them. "What happened?" "Was the bobby mad at you?"

They bug you with questions until you say it was just a case of mistaken identity and when can you eat? You're starving.

Heather thinks that on your first day in London you should do something really special, so she takes you to cream tea at the Ritz. Elizabeth goes wild over the little gold chairs and round tables with pink tablecloths, set in the fanciest room you've ever seen in your life. Golden marble columns, gold chandeliers, and floral carpet.

The food is magnificent, too—buttered scones piled high with strawberry jam and whipped cream, stacks of tiny sandwiches with no crusts.

You're glad you came here, especially after the waiter in the tailcoat brings you a third piece of chocolate fudge layer cake. Then a man in a military uniform walks by. It isn't General K, but it makes you wonder who he really was and if you should have helped him.

THE END

"I've got an idea," you say. "Any way to get inside the castle without being seen?"

Robin shakes his head. "It's high on the hill. Stone wall all around . . ."

"I've seen caves at the back of the hill," Will Scarlet says, "but I don't know if they go anywhere."

"The rocks in the wall are pretty rough," Little John suggests. "There might be footholds."

Choices: You want to try the caves (turn to page 17).

You want to try the wall (turn to page 142).

"Right-o!" The general salutes you. He looks at his watch. "I believe your friend Chris is due to meet us at that contraption we left in St. James Park."

"You brought AL here? Great!" You are so excited you almost run across the park.

"Chris! Hi!" You slap your friend on the back. "How did you get AL here? I didn't think he was programmed for Europe."

"Prof Q just got a new chip that doubles his capacity." Chris pushes the button that switches off the time machine's electronically produced invisibility.

You look around and are glad to see that no one is watching. The three of you get inside, and Chris hands you your language translators and Bible-time costumes.

"I should warn you, though. Q wasn't sure the chip was working just right. He was afraid it might stick if it got overheated, but it should do for one trip. So, what's most important, General?"

"Set this contraption for the Megiddo valley in 1240 B.C.," the general commands. "I want to see Deborah."

Turn to page 3.

The march to Jerusalem goes slowly in the great heat of midsummer. Richard rides at the head of a combined army of 10,000 men, but you wonder how many will be left by the time you get to Jerusalem. The ones who aren't killed by Arab bands sweeping down from the hills without warning are likely to succumb to sunstroke. It seems that the armor that prevents death one way is likely to cause it another.

After one sneak attack by the Turks, you see a Crusader walk by you with twenty arrows sticking in the felt padding under his chain mail.

"Would you like us to pull those arrows out for you?" you ask.

The brawny knight laughs. "I don't mind looking like a pincushion. There's not a scratch on me."

Later, after two hours of marching across the desert, the knight falls dead at your feet. His squire rushes up to remove his surcoat, hauberk of mail, and the padding under it. He was right, there wasn't a scratch on him. He was another victim of the scorching sun.

That night you think it's a great idea to make camp on the somewhat cooler bank of a river. But in the middle of the night you are wakened by horrible screams of agony. You follow men running along the riverbank with flaming torches. Everyone stops in horror as the flickering torches reveal the remains of two men who have been eaten by crocodiles.

Turn to page 88.

"Sir, there's a difference you've overlooked."

"Nonsense! A good general never overlooks anything. And I am a very good general."

"Yes, sir. But, this was in the Bible. It's not the same."

"Not the same?" the general yells. "Do you mean to say you don't believe the Bible can be relied on historically?"

"No, I mean God was helping them. Directly. So it wasn't just their military strategy."

"Nonsense!" K raps your chair with his baton.

"Well, we'll see," you say as AL settles into the sands of the Megiddo.

But instead of a raging battle, all you see when you step out is a woman with dark hair and strong features. She is sitting under a palm tree, talking to a man who wears a brown tunic and carries a sword. "I know the Canaanites are stealing all our food, but what can we do?" the man is saying.

The woman raises her arm, making her long purple mantle fall about her shoulders. "God will help us if we trust him, Barak."

Barak argues. "We don't have a chance. The Canaanites have iron-clad chariots; we have a few crude weapons."

Deborah stands tall. "This is the plan God has given me. Take ten thousand men to Mount

Tabor. General Sisera will march out to destroy us, but with God's help you can defeat them."

"I won't lead the army unless you go, too," Barak says.

"I will go. But God will deliver Israel into the hands of a woman."

Choices: You think Barak sounds cowardly, but Deborah is right (turn to page 10). You decide to follow General Sisera with his strong troops (turn to page 34).

The taller Ninja suddenly spins around and faces you. "Why do you follow me?"

"Ninja stuff is really big where I come from. I—I thought I might see you do something," you stammer.

"Come then, my American friend. I am Doron. I go to face the Test of Truth. You may watch and tell your friends in America when you return."

You go to a house. The door is open and inside is a large, bare room. Several men sit on the wooden floor—all wearing black belts on black gis. "This is *dojo*—our school," the short Ninja says as you sit. "*Godan*—Test of Truth—is very special, highly advanced stage of Ninjutsu training. In ancient days it was done with real sword, now we use *bokkun*—wooden sword."

All is quiet as Sensi, the master, stands in the center of the room with the bokkan upraised, his eyes closed. Doron sits at his feet, his back to the master, motionless—waiting. Suddenly Sensi strikes. The sword slashes down at Doron's head. Doron jerks aside, rolls, and the sword slices past.

"Hai! Yes! Godan!" the master cries.

Doron bows to his audience. "The most important thing is to keep on learning, practicing, and teaching. A real martial artist must know himself to see life clearly. First I was tense, tight; then I let go. To pass the Test of Truth, the Ninja must give himself up."

You think about it as you walk to Paddington.

Turn to page 16.

You turn around and are so surprised you have to blink three times. "Chris!" you yell. Then, because you're still so surprised to see your old friend, you flop down in the grass. Chris flops down beside you.

"What are *you* doing here?" you ask.

"Looking for you." Chris chews on a blade of grass. "That is, we were, but we gave up and come to Nottinghamshire because some World War I dude was born here and General K wanted to see if his family was still around—"

"Wait a minute!" You roll over and punch your friend in the arm. "*Why* were you looking for me? We *who*? General *what*?"

Chris laughs and socks you back. "*We* are me and General Kempthorne. He's very big with NATO?"

"What's NATO?"

Chris looks superior. "North Atlantic Treaty Organization—a defense treaty between the U.S., England, West Germany, Italy, Holland, and a bunch of others. It's probably the reason Western Europe is free today and that there hasn't been World War III."

"Oh."

"I know, because General Kempthorne works with them. He told me."

"Yeah, but you haven't told me who this General K guy is."

"He hired AL from Prof. Q to go back in history and study great battles. Here he comes now."

Turn to page 102.

Before dawn you are getting ready to ride with Napoleon. "I'll take Miss Beth in the saddle with me," says General K, who has commandeered horses from Napoleon's stables. "The rest of you must keep up."

"Right-o!" You salute the general. Napoleon may command the cavalry, but you know who commands you.

Nearby, the top of Mount Tabor reflects the sunrise as you ride out.

"Onward, my children!" Napoleon shouts from the head of the line. "In the name of the Goddess of Liberty, great riches shall be ours today!"

You see the enemy—masses of Turks—below as you sweep into the valley. You are outnumbered 12 to one, yet Napoleon charges forward without a break and gives the order to attack. From the middle of the cavalry charge you can't see much that's going on. But you hear the

bloodcurdling yells of the Turks as they hew and slash with their razor-sharp swords.

Against all impossibilities, the French break through the Turkish defense and open fire. The enemy falls by the hundreds. Seeing the battle lost, the Turks ride off into the desert.

Now the French soldiers are rewarded for their bravery. The Turks carry all their wealth with them, so many of the dead bodies littering the sand are carrying gold and jewels worth a small fortune. French soldiers begin looting the bodies. But Napoleon rides off to his victory dinner.

Choices: You want a share of the gold and jewels (turn to page 120).
You follow Napoleon to dinner (turn to page 43).

"Sir Balin!" you shout.

When he looks up, you toss him the sword you took from the fallen Crusader.

"Thank 'ee!" Balin cries and turns to strike a Turk about to make a fatal cut with his scimitar.

You glance toward Richard, who is fighting valiantly, driving three of Saladin's men before the sweeps of his sword. But then you see a fourth attacker at his back. You are weaponless.

"Richard! Look out!" you shout, but the king doesn't hear you.

There's only one chance as the Turk raises his glinting, curved weapon. You kick both heels into your horse and charge at the enemy. Your horse crashes into the Turk's with the force of a bulldozer, and you are both flung to the ground.

You come to on a bed of red and gold silk cushions and you smell spices and sweet cakes. All is peaceful and quiet. You turn over with a groan. You must have been killed in battle. This must be Heaven. You'll never see your folks and Lizard again.

Then the tent flaps open, and King Richard the Lionheart strides in. "This day in battle you saved the life of your sovereign. I do not know you, but Sir Kempthorne calls you American."

You slip to your knees before Richard as he raises his sword above your head, then brings it down to tap each shoulder lightly.

When you rise, Chris kneels before you and kisses your hand. "I shall be your squire."

THE END

The victorious troops gather around Deborah, who stands in the middle of the Hebrew army and sings:

"Praise ye the Lord for the avenging of Israel,
I will sing praise to the Lord God of Israel.
The earth trembled, and the heavens dropped water.
So let all your enemies perish, O Lord."

You can't resist making one last comment to the general, "*She* doesn't seem to think it was a coincidence."

But the general isn't listening to you, and no one else is either. Barak and many of the men are singing and dancing with Deborah in an act of worship. Others are dragging up supply carts captured from the enemy, laden with more food and provisions than the starving Israelites have seen for months.

The rain has quit, and you join others of the Hebrews in cooking a great feast. As the smell of roasting meat fills the air, and baskets of honey cakes, cheeses, and dates are served to you again and again, you know that you are thankful that it rained today—whether or not it would have anyway. Or did God tell Deborah to choose today because he knew it was gong to rain?

THE END

Chris turns toward the door, then stops. "There he is—over here, General!"

Everyone looks at you as Chris shouts, but the tall man in the khaki-colored uniform with all the medals on his chest strides forward without the least bit of embarrassment.

You wonder if you should salute, but he offers to shake hands. "General Kempthorne, British Army," he says.

"British Army?" you ask, after you've stammered your name. "I thought Chris said the Pentagon called?"

"Yes, I am attached to the Pentagon with NATO, so there's no question of divided loyalties, my young American friend."

"No, no. Of course not. What battle do you want to study?"

"I should like to start in Old Testament times with Deborah and the strategy she gave Barak."

"Oh." You've been thinking so much about the Crusades, it's hard to change ideas. "Where was that?"

"In the Meddigo Valley, north of Jerusalem, near the Sea of Galilee."

You're still looking at a massive two-handed sword that the sign beside it says might have been carried by King Richard on the third Crusade. "Could we see something else in that same place first?"

The general nods. "All of Esdraelon is of interest—it is the battlefield of history, the cockpit of the human race. The entire plain is stained with the blood of the armies of history. Just take me there—to any time you choose."

Choices: You take the general to Deborah (turn to page 3).

You follow your crusading interests (turn to page 132).

"Excellent strategy. Surprise is the essence. Also her personality is magnetic, inspiring, forceful. Just what we need." K turns and strides up the mountain toward Deborah. You scramble after him, listening to him talk to himself.

"Wait! What do you mean—'just what we need'?" You trip over a loose rock and fall. Your knee burns like fire, and blood is dripping onto your toes, but you ignore it. "General . . ."

Too late—he's already approaching the prophetess. You're watching helplessly when Chris joins you.

"What's K doing?"

"He's got some crazy idea of taking her back."

"Back? To our time?"

"He said something about her being able to inspire people who vote against military spending. Do you think he's bonkers?"

"If he thinks we can take her back, he is."

There's nothing you can do but wait—and mop up the blood drying on your leg. At least rainwater's clean to wash with.

"Let's go."

You look up to see a curious expression on General K's face. "She won't leave her people. But she said the strangest thing—"

"What?" you and Chris ask at the same time.

"She said 'righteousness alone exhalteth a nation.' What do you suppose she meant by that?"

You and Chris grin at each other.

THE END

From the boulder where you are still sprawled, you see Sisera's iron chariots sink into the mire and watch the Israelites attack the trapped enemy with speed and courage.

"Well, what do you think about miracles now?" you ask General K, who is standing near you trying to take notes on his soggy paper.

"Amazing coincidence," he says.

Choices: You think the general could be right (turn to page 85).

You think the general is obviously wrong (turn to page 59).

You're not sure what to think (turn to page 62).

AL takes you to December of 1192. Richard has won the battle of Asuf, but Saladin refuses to surrender Jerusalem. You hear Richard's men grumbling, but no matter how sick and tired they are, they will follow where Richard the Lionheart leads.

A short time later, however, even the valiant Richard has to stop. The rain begins slowly, and you couldn't be happier.

"WOW! Just feel that cool, moist air!"

"Yeah, and we won't have to worry about getting thirsty!" Chris agrees.

But pretty soon the mud get hard to walk in. Even your imitation armor makes walking harder; you can imagine what it's doing to the Crusaders, who are wearing heavy chain mail. A horse just ahead of you steps in a puddle and sinks up to his knees.

Choices: You help pull the horse out (turn to page 68). (turn to page 68)
You keep on slogging through the mud (turn to page 124). (turn to page 124)

Allenby's troops cover more than seventy miles in thirty-four hours. Elizabeth sleeps in the saddle in front of K and eats chocolate bars from the officers.

All you can do is hang on and spit the sand out of your mouth. You just grit your teeth and think how nice it will be when you get to Damascus: cold drinks, warm bath, soft bed. . . .

You pause outside the gates of the ancient city while Allenby listens to a report. "It's as I feared," he says. "Disease is rampant."

"What! We aren't going in there, are we?" you yell.

"One has a duty." Allenby rides forward.

That night Elizabeth wakes up burning with fever. After she vomits for the third time, you know you have to do something. "Has penicillin been invented yet?" you ask.

"Afraid not," Chris says. "Nine years from now in 1928. I got it right on a science test."

"Oh, great! And AL's in Megiddo." You try to think, but Elizabeth keeps whimpering, and your brain won't work. Elizabeth starts muttering and you go over to her.

"Now I lay me down to sleep," she whispers. "I pray the Lord my soul to keep."

Turn to page 141.

Still trying not to let your mouth hang open, you are escorted up a stone and marble arched stairway to an equally impressively vaulted room. It's lined with marble busts that the bobby say are of England's prime ministers.

"You was askin' for this person, sir?" Your guide speaks to a man in some kind of military uniform, and then leaves you alone.

"I am General Kempthorne," the tall man with a dark mustache says. "I need to go back into time on a matter of some national importance. Your friend Professor Quinten tells me you possess the skills I require."

You look at his uniform. You aren't sure what it is, but you know it isn't American. He said national importance—but which nation?

Choices: You say, "If Q says it's okay, it's okay with me" (turn to page 49).

You say, "I think I'd like to check with the American embassy, first" (turn to page 128).

You say, "I'm sorry, but I can't just run off and leave my sister" (turn to page 47).

The room is quiet, except for the crackling fire. Thirty-three pairs of eyes are looking at you.

"Um, er—once upon a time . . . there was a rooster, named, er—Chanticleer. He was beautiful and proud. One day a fox came out of the woods and said, 'I remember your father—what a gorgeous creature he was! He used to hold his head up and stand on his toes and sing from the depths of his heart. In his greatest moments he closed his eyes. . . . Ah, he was wonderful. I wonder, can his son do so well?'

"Well, now, old Chanticleer wasn't about to be outdone by his dad, so he did just what the fox said—even closed his eyes. As soon as he did, the fox grabbed him and dragged him off with the whole barnyard following.

"Now Chanticleer was plenty scared, but he thought fast. 'When we get to the woods,' he told the fox, 'if I were you, I'd turn around and yell na-ya-na-ya-na-ya!'

"And that's exactly what the fox did. And as soon as he opened his mouth, Chanticleer flew off. Er, the end." You bow.

Everyone applauds—everyone but Chaucer, who's too busy writing down what you said. You suddenly realize that your story is going to become part of a piece of great literature. You'll study your own story in English class! Not bad.

Uh-oh. You look at Lizard, who is still clapping. She's going to bug you to tell her a story every night.

THE END

The horse is a long-legged gray with a black mane and tail. He is terrified of the storm and of being trapped in the mud. He tosses his head up and tries to lunge and rear when you attempt to help him. Then, finding himself stuck fast, he thrashes harder.

"Look out, he'll bite," his owner yells, when you try to grasp the side of his bridle and pull his head forward.

The situation looks hopeless, because the harder the horse struggles, the deeper in the mud he sinks.

"We can't just go off and leave him," you yell above the slosh of the rain and the sucking sound of warriors pulling their feet out of the mire.

Suddenly the ground under you gives way. Chris grabs you. You watch openmouthed as water and mud drain away into the hole that has opened up in the ground where you were standing two seconds before.

As the puddle empties, the horse is able to pull his legs free, and he and his master move ahead with the Crusaders.

But you stand, peering into the cave. "Wish we could see in."

You've no more than spoken when a sheet of lightning fills the sky with light. It only lasts a second, but it's long enough. "There's something in there!" you yell. "I'm going to get it!"

Turn to page 110.

Turn to page 125.

AL's chronograph tells you you've arrived in Canterbury four days after Christmas in the year 1170 A.D. Elizabeth and Heather still don't believe what you've told them about AL, but when they step out and see a completely different looking cathedral, they begin to be convinced.

"There was a fire in 1174, and the cathedral rebuilt after that—but I don't understand." Heather shakes her head.

Before you can explain more, you hear angry shouts and the clanking of armor. You turn toward the arch behind you in time to see four fully armed knights, clad in heavy chain mail hauberks to their knees, storming into the cathedral grounds. They're followed by an excited mob shaking sticks and throwing stones.

The tallest knight, carrying a shield with a rampant bear and wielding a long-bladed, heavy sword, passes within inches of you. He doesn't see you, but you get a good look at him. The look in his eyes is one of pure murder.

You're responsible for the safety of Heather and Elizabeth—and this is *not* a safe place.

Choices: You hide in the cathedral (turn to page 8).

You get back in AL (turn to page 130).

You look around for some kind of a weapon and seize a golden candlestick. On a bench near it is a monk's cloak which you slip on, pulling the cowl over your head. Frightened monks run away, as you rush forward.

But you are too late. The bear cub knight leaps upon Thomas and wounds him on the head. The archbishop falls to the floor. You drop your useless weapon and slip to your knees, holding Thomas's bleeding head.

"We are not here to triumph by fighting or by resistance, nor to fight with men as beasts," he says. "This is the easier victory. Now is the triumph of the Cross!"

The next blow silences the archbishop and cuts a searing gap in your arm that cradles his head.

THE END

Chris goes off to test AL. Heather and Elizabeth find you, and Elizabeth is all excited. "Heather's going to take us to the best toy store in the world!"

Heather nods. "Hamley's. Their motto is 'The World's Finest Toy Store,' and I think you'll agree with them."

You do. You can't decide whether to watch the puppet show in front of you, the wind-up toys under your feet, or the electric train running above your head. Every toy in the world has its own section, with a video story about it showing on TV. Elizabeth takes off to the My Little Ponys and Flower Fairies. You check out the Transformers and Masters of the Universe, but the Lego display really grabs you. At the entrance is a knight in armor almost as tall as you—built entirely of Legos. His armor is gray, his gold shield and breastplate have a white bird on

them. And at his feet is a white dog—also built of Legos.

Farther back is a fortified medieval castle with little Lego knights defending the battlements—scaling ladders, drawing bows, manning catapults—all moving. You watch a team outside the wall repeatedly smash a battering ram against the gates.

Suddenly you feel really dumb—why should you be standing in a toy store watching little plastic brick people when you could be living the real thing?

"I'll meet you back at the hotel," you call to Heather, and run out the door before she can try to stop you.

You find Chris and General K looking for you outside the Tower.

"Seems to work OK," Chris says about AL.

Turn to page 132.

General Kempthorne is pacing back and forth in front of a Crusader tent, waving a stick like a baton. "I'll not be kept here cooling my heels!"

"No, sir. Er, yes, sir," Chris says.

"Haven't used siege warfare for 150 years. This is no help!" He whacks the tent with his stick.

"Yes, sir." This time Chris salutes.

The general sees you. "So there you are. Into that infernal contraption—there's work to do!"

"Yes, sir." You sound like Chris.

"To the battle of Arsuf, near Jerusalem," K commands when you're inside AL. "Next summer."

Turn to page 89.

For a while you follow Elizabeth's sobs and the sound of the men crashing through the woods, but the bandits know the territory and you don't. Finally you plop down on a tree stump and drop your head in your hands.

"It's hopeless! What are we gonna do, Chris? I thought she was such a brat, but all of a sudden—you know, I really *care*. I mean, she's not so bad, as little sisters go. Chris, you're not listening to me—"

Chris holds up his hand. "Shhh, listen—"

Through the trees behind you comes the sound of church bells ringing. "A church? Maybe we can get help there!" You jump up and start running. Fortunately the bells keep ringing to guide you to the village of Blidworth. Beside the village green is a pretty little house where a young woman is cutting flowers in the garden.

"May I help you?" she asks. "My name is Marian."

"*Maid Marian*?"

When she nods, you tell her about Elizabeth's kidnapping.

"How terrible! But never fear, my dear Robin Hood can rescue her." She calls a servant and you all go into the forest again to find Robin's men.

Turn to page 134.

The archbishop's voice rings through the cathedral. "I am ready to die for my Lord and for the sake of liberty and peace. But in the name of Almighty God, I forbid you to harm my people!" He bows his head and lifts his hands in prayer.

You grab Elizabeth and turn her face away from the scene as the first blow falls across Thomas à Becket's head. Another blow falls on a monk who holds the archbishop in his arms.

"For the name of Jesus, I am ready to embrace death," Thomas cries, just before the final blow silences him.

A knight puts his foot on Thomas's neck and yells, "Let us away, knights; he will rise no more!"

Choices: You follow the knights (turn to page 83).

You stay there (turn to page 121).

According to your arrangements, the two leaders meet in Saladin's sumptuous gold and purple tent, which is draped with silk and filled with tasseled cushions. Servants present platters of fruit and cheeses and offer spiced drinks in golden goblets. Since you are with Richard, you are served, too.

Then they get down to business. Saladin agrees to give Christian pilgrims to the Holy Land safe conduct to Jerusalem and to allow the Crusaders to keep Acre and all the country they have conquered. Jerusalem will stay in Saracen control.

"I will return some time to conquer the Holy Land," Richard says.

The Saracen replies, "If I must lose the Holy Land, there is no one to whom I would rather lose it than the English King."

THE END

It's pouring rain when you get off the train in Canterbury. But above the pattering drops on your hood and the splashing of cars on the street, you hear the clear, beautiful chimes of bells ringing from the cathedral. You look up through the curtain of water and see the great, square bell tower dominating the skyline high above the trees.

"The medieval builders wanted to create a reflection of God's Heaven on earth," Heather says. "I like to think of the cathedral as prayers in stone. There has been a church here since 592 A.D. when St. Augustine was first Archbishop of Canterbury."

While Heather talks, you walk under an archway spanning the street and enter the cathedral "close," the area between the building and the outer wall. You stop and stare. You had no idea a building could make you forget to breathe.

"Move!" Elizabeth yells, jabbing you between

the shoulder blades with her umbrella. There is a big puddle in front of you, so to avoid another jab from Lizard you jump . . . and bounce back smack on your bottom in the rain puddle. You sit there, rubbing your head and trying to figure out what you hit. You sure can't see anything.

You get up and move slowly, groping. You touch something—smooth, curved metal. Is it possible? A bit more searching and you find it— AL's invisibility button. You give it a flip and there it is—Prof Q's time machine. You couldn't be more surprised, but finding AL gives you an idea. . . .

Choices: You decide to take Heather and Elizabeth back into Canterbury's history (turn to page 74).
You wait around for Chris, who must have come with AL (turn to page 137).

There is great excitement in Robin's camp when you return and tell about the treasure. "Sounds like some of Prince John's tax collectors are holding out on him. Stealing from thieves will be more fun than stealing from the rich!" Robin slaps you on the back and laughs.

"And giving it to King Richard to defeat the infidel is as holy a cause as giving to the poor." Friar Tuck's mischievous grin sparks his pious words.

You lead the men to the cave and the next morning wave away a band of "pilgrims" as Robin's men leave to take the treasure to their king.

"Pretty tricky," Chris says.

"Huh?" you ask.

"Helping Richard win the war is the best way to secure his throne for him."

"You think so?"

General K answers. "No doubt about it. No one will be loyal to John when they can have a hero like Richard for king. You should stick around till he comes back—you could have any reward you ask for."

"Hmmm," you say. "I'll think about it."

THE END

You and Heather catch Elizabeth at the same time. "Don't ever run off like that again!" you start to lecture, but just then a life-size Paddington Bear walks by in his big, floppy hat. You have to admit he's pretty neat.

While Elizabeth goes up to hug him and drop her shilling in the can he's carrying to collect money for blind children, Heather asks where you want to go—Nottingham or Canterbury?

Elizabeth saw the Walt Disney Robin Hood on TV last month, and you know she's wild to go to Sherwood Forest and pretend she's Maid Marian. But you read a book in school last year about Canterbury—how Thomas à Becket was murdered there, how all the pilgrims went there on trips in the Middle Ages, and how the Black Prince was buried there. . . .

Choices: You ask for Nottingham (turn to page 138).

You want Canterbury (turn to page 78).

You are all taken in a police limousine up a wide boulevard with parkland on both sides. You drive around a huge fountain and through ornate black and gold metal gates.

"Buckingham Palace," your escort from Scotland Yard tells you.

Inside, you walk down long marble corridors past rows of uniformed, bowing footmen. You are ushered into a room with gold-framed paintings and elegant gold furniture grouped on red carpets.

"Wait here," a servant says.

In a few moments the doors open again, and a beautiful woman in a soft green dress and a diamond tiara comes in. "Her Majesty, the Queen," a footman announces, and presents you to Queen Elizabeth II.

Your sister curtsies and you bow. "Hello, Your Majesty." You've never been so thankful in all your life for your mother's manners lectures.

"I understand you prevented my jewels from being stolen today." The queen looks at you with a sparkling smile.

You bow again. "Yes, Your Majesty."

"I wish to reward you." She raises her hand, and a servant steps up holding a silver tray. "The royal sceptre. Only a replica, of course."

"*Thank you, Your Majesty!*" You don't care if it's a copy—it looks great!

"And for you—" She holds a replica of the

Imperial State Crown out to your sister.

"I didn't really do anything, Your Majesty," Elizabeth says.

"I know. But since we have the same name I wanted you to have something, too."

You know you'll never call her Lizard again.

THE END

Nottingham is a busy industrial city, but as you climb the high rocky hill to the castle you feel the centuries melt away. Outside the castle walls is a life-size bronze statue of Robin Hood with his bow drawn. You stand before it and read the plaque: "In merry England in the time of old, there lived within the green glades of Sherwood Forest, near Nottingham Town, a famous outlaw whose name was Robin Hood. No archer ever lived with such skill and cunning as his, nor were there ever such yeomen as the merry men that roamed with him through the greenwood shades. . . ."

You close your eyes and you really are back in the Middle Ages. Well—almost. "Boy! I wish Chris were here with AL!"

You don't realize you've spoken aloud until an army officer steps up and salutes you. "You are Chris's friend? I also have that honor. I can take you to him."

But even after you find Chris, who explains that he and General Kempthorne have come to get you to fly AL on a mission, you still find it hard to believe.

"But I can wait," says the general. "You three youngsters go see Robin Hood while this charming lady and I share a pot of tea." The general bows to Heather.

"All right! What a plan!" You run down the hill to AL with Chris and Elizabeth.

Turn to page 28.

"Well, maybe—" you start to say. Then a figure moving at the edge of the battlefield catches your attention. "Is that Sisera?"

The general adjusts his field glasses in the direction you're pointing. "Why, so it is."

"Let's follow him." You jump to your feet and wave to Chris to come. You circle around the sunken chariots, thrashing horses, and bleeding Canaanite soldiers, stepping on rocks as much as possible to avoid getting stuck knee deep in the mud. All the time, you strain to keep your eyes on the fleeing figure in a gold-trimmed purple tunic. A weak sun comes out after the rain, making your job easier as it glimmers on Sisera's bronze helmet.

But it also makes you uncomfortable as the warmth turns the soggy desert into a sauna.

"Isn't that guy going to get tired?" Chris pants at your side.

"I don't think generals ever rest," you say, looking at General K, who is striding ahead of you, not even perspiring.

But at the edge of the village of Kedesh, Sisera stops before a rich-looking tent. You are just behind him when a woman in a blue and gold robe comes out of the tent and bows.

"Come in; do not be afraid. I am Jael, wife of one of your king's allies." She holds the tent flap back for Sisera to enter. Then she sees you. "Come," she calls. "Help me serve this man."

Choices: You go to help her (turn to page 11). You back off (turn to page 22).

You start to open the door, but the general barks at you to wait. "In a military operation, you do not proceed until ordered!"

You sit quietly while the general questions Chris about the working of the chronograph, which moves you in time, and the cartograph, which moves you in space.

"The superior officer must always know the equipment of the troops," he says. You'd like to explain that you aren't one of his troops, but instead you just shrug.

General K practices setting the dials himself, supervised by you and Chris. Then he tucks a pair of large field glasses inside his robe and swings the door open.

You are hit in the face with a flood of water and hail blown in by a gust of wind. As you reel back into your seat, a cavalry charge rushes by on both sides, nearly toppling AL into the mud. You look down. "Oh, no! AL's sinking! Move us out of here!"

You slam the door, and Chris sets the gauges. Nothing.

"Hurry!" you yell. "We're gonna drown in mud!"

"Can't move him," Chris says.

"What do you mean, can't move?"

"I guess the Prof. was wrong when he thought the chip would be safe for one trip. The cartograph's gone." Chris stares at the blank screen. You feel AL settle deeper in the slime.

"Doesn't anything work?" General K demands.

Your screen is still bright. "Chronograph is fine. We can move in time."

"Well, then, what are you waiting for? Set it for today!"

"Yes, sir." You salute. It's probably the only thing to do, but it's going to be a long walk back to London.

THE END

You turn to Chris, but he isn't there. You haven't seen him since early evening when he went for a walk along the river.

"Chris! Chris!" You run up and down shouting until General K holds you and makes you stop.

He holds out a familiar object. Chris's voice translator. "I found it in the, er, remains," he says.

"No, no!" You start hitting and kicking and screaming until the general grabs you again.

"That won't help anything," he says.

"I know. Nothing can help. Ever." Then you realize that isn't quite true. At least you've always been taught that God could help in any situation. . . .

Choices: You pray (turn to page 39).

You go for a walk (turn to page 31).

If the general wanted action, you've arrived at the right moment. Saladin has amassed a huge army on the plain of Arsuf to meet Richard's hundred thousand men. The sun burns from above and the sands from below, but the mighty armies are unchecked.

Just as you step out of AL, a band of swift Arab horsemen sweep toward Richard's marching column, shouting, "Allah is great! Allah is great! There is no god but Allah!"

Richard, on his mighty white war-horse, turns to the attackers, raises his gleaming longsword, and cries, "Saint George for England!" The Crusaders charge.

Richard is everywhere, his great sword carving a lane of dead wherever he rides, inspiring his warriors. The air resounds with drums and trumpets; banners whip in the wind. The excitement of battle seizes you. You start to rush forward on foot when a Crusader near you falls from his horse, an arrow piercing his mail. You grab his weapon and horse and swing into the saddle.

"For God and Saint George!" you cry.

You charge into the battle near Richard, a shower of arrows falling around you. Sir Balin, a knight fighting just behind Richard, is nicked in the wrist by an arrow—not enough to wound him, but enough to make him drop his sword.

Choices: You toss him your sword (turn to page 58).
You charge forward (turn to page 19).

Don't let it be sealed, you pray.

Without even a creak, the trapdoor springs up so sharply it throws you over backwards. Blood, caught mid-leap in his lunge at the jewel case, falls neatly down the trap.

"Bravo!" The guide springs forward to help you slam the hatch. You can hear Blood howling from below.

Suddenly there is banging on the door. "It's locked!"

Your guide grins and pulls an enormous black iron key out of her pocket.

The bobbies rush in. "Where is he?"

You point to the trapdoor. Most of the constables run down the stairs, but one stays to interview you. Still massaging your bruised bottom, you tell him what you did.

"I'm sorry you ran into a spot of bother on your first day in London," the bobby says. "But if you'll just come with me, I know someone who'll want to thank you."

Turn to page 82.

The steep, rocky pass is rugged and foreboding. In the dim light of early morning, you think you see an ambush behind every boulder. But you pass through without incident and come out on the well-traveled road known as The Way of the Sea. At times you glimpse the shining blue Mediterranean to your right.

As you travel, a pilgrim named John of Macintyre tells you of his journey from Scotland: first to Rome to visit the graves of the apostles, then by sea to Constantinople, and now—the ultimate in his holy journey—to Jerusalem, the City of God. John's face glows as he tells about his adventures and their religious significance.

The first night, you camp in the desert under the stars with Knights Templar standing guard. But the second night you find a comfortable inn inside a walled city. You barely have time to wash the dust of the road off your tired feet when Chris comes in.

"Big doings tonight—we're local celebrities. Sultan al-Kamil has invited us to his palace, and Saladin's brother Malek el Adil sends greetings to those who wish to call on him."

"I thought the Turks were the enemy," you say. "You suppose it's a trap?"

Choices: You visit Sultan al-Kamil (turn to page 96).

You go to see Saladin's brother (turn to page 94).

You get out of there (turn to page 22).

"The Tower of London is over 900 years old and is our most famous historic building," Heather says as you enter the massive brick wall through Traitor's Gate. "This is the same gate the young Elizabeth was brought through when her sister, was queen—about 400 years ago."

"Elizabeth, just like me?"

You're still so glad your sister wasn't hit by that car, you don't even say a thing.

"Yes, Elizabeth, just like you." Heather smiles at her. "But she refused to go in. 'I am no traitor,' she said and sat down in the pouring rain. She knew her mother had been executed in the Tower, and she thought she might be."

"Was she?" Elizabeth looks a little pale.

"No. Her sister wasn't very healthy and she died five years later. Elizabeth became queen then. She had to stay at the tower again the night before her coronation, but she never came here after that."

"Was she a good queen?"

"Elizabeth reigned for forty-five years and was one of the best rulers England ever had."

Your sister looks smug at Heather's answer.

"Now," Heather says, "shall we go to the Jewel House or the Armory?"

"Oh, please, the jewels." Elizabeth begs.

Choices: You say, "You two go on, I'm going to see the armor" (turn to page 126).
You say, "Sure, I'd like to see the crown jewels, as long as we can see the armor later (turn to page 104).

Sir Byron, the handsomest of your Templar escorts, leads those of you who choose to pay your respects to the brother of Saladin to a villa on a hillside surrounded by olive orchards.

The villa of Malek el Adil is draped with colorful silks and woven tapestries. You are invited to lounge on a thick Persian carpet and sip a sweet fruit drink. Musicians play pipes and stringed instruments softly in the background.

The emperor's brother and King Richard's knight face each other with every show of courtesy—much bowing and many polite words—but you can see they are eyeing each other warily. Malek wears a large silk turban like a pillow on his head, flowing blue and scarlet robes, and light, embroidered slippers. He has rings on his fingers, and the scabbard at his side is studded with gems.

Sir Bryon's heavy boots and thick, plain shirt and pants look out of place, but it is his long, two-handed sword that attracts Malek's attention. He suggests a contest.

Byron's mighty weapon looks clumsy next to the curved razor-sharp scimitar of Malek. But Byron raises it over his head and with a single, clanging blow, cuts an iron bar in half.

It is Malek el Adil's turn. He tosses a fine silk scarf into the air and cuts it cleanly in two.

Each weapon is perfect in its own way. You wonder why the armies can't leave it at that and let each nation live in its own way.

THE END

The marines make the room shrink to about half the size it seemed before.

"May I see your passport?" Michaels holds out his hand.

You dig in your pocket and hand the little blue book to him.

"Hmmm" is all he says.

Then he snaps his fingers. The marines move to each side of you, and Michaels stands. "General Kempthorne is engaged in a top-secret information-gathering operation. NATO is very curious as to why *you* are asking questions about *him.* I'm afraid I'll have to detain you while we look into just what your interest in him is. And why you were talking to the entrance guard about Russian architecture."

The marines pull you to your feet.

"What! Wait a minute! You can't do this to— I'm an American citizen!"

Michaels smiles at you coldly. "Precisely."

THE END

A small group of you, led by a monk pilgrim named Brother Francis, walk through the narrow, twisting passages choked with children, goats, and donkeys to the Sultan's palace. Inside the high white walls you find peace and beauty in the graceful building with flowing arches, white pillars, and mosaic-tiled floors.

The sultan serves you fruit and goat's cheese. After a bit of polite dialogue, Brother Francis leads the conversation around to tell Sultan al-Kamil about Christ, the son of the Holy One of Israel. He tells about the miracles he performed right in the country you are traveling through and the faith in the one true God he proclaimed.

"There is no God but Allah," the Sultan replies.

"Your highness, let me make a proposal: Let

me and the Saracen holy man walk through fire together. If I emerge unharmed, as I am certain I will, it will prove that the religion of Christ is the only true faith."

Al-Kamil slowly eats a grape and then shakes his head. "Friar, I do not think that any Saracen would wish to go through fire for his faith. But pray for me that God may choose to show me the law and the faith that are most pleasing to him."

Now you realize the importance of the monks' work here—faith like that of Brother Francis can do far more to win the Holy Land for Christendom than all the might of the Crusaders.

THE END

Thankful for the deep shadows in the narrow passages between the tents, you dive into a dark hole and pull the loose tent fabric over your head. Not daring to breathe, you lie still for a long time—long after you hear the guards slip past you in the soft sand.

When you start breathing again, you realize the men in the tent on the other side of the fabric wall from you are awake and talking in hushed voices. You turn on Prof Q's instant language translator and listen.

"We will destroy the French tomorrow. That Napoleon, he does not know our strength, nor our valor."

You hold your breath again. This is what you were sent to hear. "The French general has only 1500 men in the Megiddo Valley. His horsemen are laughable—maybe 600. We are 25,000. Tomorrow we will end the French invasion!"

It sounds bad, but Napoleon needs to know. You crawl out into the sand and motion to Chris. "Did you hear?"

He nods, "Yeah, I heard. Let's get outa here—I mean, get our friends and get clear out."

Choices: You decide to go on with Napoleon (turn to page 56).
You fly AL to safety (turn to page 100).

You jump off the bus and run over a low hill where, almost magically, you find a little country fair with lights shining and music playing from what Heather calls a roundabout, but you call a merry-go-round.

The first thing Elizabeth wants is cotton candy. You get a bag of popcorn.

"Yuck! They put sugar on this!" You use it to feed the birds.

Elizabeth wants to ride on the sledge swing. " 'Cept it looks scary," she says.

"Okay," you say. "I'll go with you."

The swings are suspended from high, painted wooden frames. Elizabeth chooses the pink one. You climb up the ladder and sit on benches facing each other. The man running the ride propels the swing by pulling a rope. Soon you have the feeling of flying over the little dale next to the forest.

"Not bad for a kid's ride," you say when you get off. Heather tells you that 200 years ago those were a favorite entertainment of fashionable ladies.

Elizabeth wants to jump in the inflated castle, but you say, "No, thanks. I'll meet you at the Visitors' Center."

You're halfway across the meadow when you hear someone calling your name—but he can't mean you. No one here knows your name.

Choices: You turn around (turn to page 55).
          You keep walking (turn to page 133).

You slip back to Napoleon's camp and gather your group—but the general won't leave.

"I came to see battles and I'm not leaving until I've seen one."

When you tell him how outnumbered Napoleon is, he wants to see it all the more. "That's exactly the kind of situation I want to observe. I won't learn anything new by watching generals that have everything going for them."

"Okay," you say. "We'll come back for you, but I want to get my sister to safety."

You and Chris set your gauges and push buttons. Outside you can hear the stomping and snorting of Napoleon's cavalry.

"Hurry up! Move this thing!" you yell at Chris.

"I'm trying. Nothing's happening!"

"What do you mean?"

Chris groans, "Prof Q told me there was a chance the new chip he put in could go out. It was working fine up till now."

Outside a battle horn sounds, and AL vibrates with the shaking earth. "Move this thing! We're in the path of the cavalry charge!" you yell.

AL begins to bounce and teeter. The charging army is only a few feet away. "Look out!" you yell, covering your head.

Elizabeth takes off her shoe and whacks AL's computer. Suddenly you don't hear any horses.

You open the door carefully, and then lean back. "Good job, Lizard. You brought us down on top of Big Ben. Now what?"

THE END

You jump to your feet and salute the tall military figure striding toward you.

"Kempthorne, in Her Majesty's service," he introduces himself.

He holds out a map of the Holy Land and points to a small triangle area near the top of the page. "This is where I want to go—the Megiddo Valley on the Plain of Esdraelon. In the history of the world, more important battles have been fought there than any other spot on the globe."

"And you've got AL here?" you ask.

"Right by that oak tree." Chris points to the edge of the forest and starts walking.

You grin foolishly. "Oh, yeah. It's been so long I'd forgotten about the invisibility capability. And you brought voice translators and Bible-time costumes?"

"Lots of costumes. General K wants to go to a bunch of different times."

Back in your old seat in AL, you locate the general's map on AL's cartograph and push the button.

Nothing happens.

"Oh, no," Chris groans. "Q put in a new chip so AL could fly to Europe. We *thought* it would work."

"Well, if we can still move in time, let's just go back to Robin Hood's day," you suggest. "I'd like to see Prince John. I've always wondered if he was as bad a king as the stories make him out to be."

Turn to page 12.

The knights hurry back to the court of King Henry. At the far end of the royal reception room, amid the lesser nobles and servants, you watch as the knights report their deed. Instead of giving them the reward they expected, Henry thunders at them.

"What! You killed my minister? My friend?" He tears his purple robe off and bows his head. "It's my fault. I accept the blame—all because of a few hasty words. What a tragic mistake."

Then Henry stands and faces his court. "I will make amends. The property we seized from Canterbury shall be returned, and I shall visit the tomb of Saint Thomas to suffer penance. I shall bear punishment for my share of the crime. And I vow further—for this heinous act, I shall go on a holy crusade."

Aha! That strikes you as a great idea. If you could only find Chris, and take Heather and Elizabeth back to London, you could go on a crusade. Not with King Henry—you're not too sure he ever carried through on that. You want to go with his son, Richard the Lionheart.

Turn to page 108.

You enter the Jewel House and go up a narrow, winding, stone stairway. In the center of the room at the top is a glass case, and inside the case, under dazzling lights, is one of the world's most valuable jewel collections.

The guide points to a ruby the size of a golf ball in the front of a crown. "That is the Black Prince's ruby, given him by Pedro the Cruel, King of Castile, after they won a great battle. The diamond below the ruby is one of the Stars of Africa. The larger Star is in the sceptre."

"Has anyone ever tried to rob this place?" you ask.

"In 1671 Colonel Thomas Blood overpowered the guard—who was seventy-seven years old and unarmed. Blood made off with some jewels, but was stopped just outside the Tower."

"Did they hang him?" you ask.

"No! Charles II rewarded him. He liked Blood's daring and thought he would be useful as a spy."

Suddenly the large wooden door to the room slams shut, and a raucous laugh echoes off the stone walls.

"I thank yer for the introduction. Colonel Blood's me ancestor, and I'm here to finish what he started!"

"Don't worry," the guide whispers, "it's electronically protected."

"*Was,* yer mean!" Blood laughs again. "Until about five minutes ago, when me mates took over the computers."

Blood swings a heavy battle-ax over his head.

Is he threatening you or preparing to break the glass case?

As he steps forward, you see a metal ring in the floor. Do you dare?

Choices: You stay against the wall (turn to page 123).

You grab the ring and jerk it up (turn to page 90).

Before you open AL's door Chris, asks, "When is it?"

You shrug. "Don't know. I just turned the dial as far as it would go. You want the future, I'll give you the future." You yank the door open.

"Wait, I just remembered—" General K starts to say, but stops in horror as a band of men walk by in front of you. They are covered from head to foot with disgusting, running sores.

"One of them touched me!" Chris shudders. "Quick, I've got to wash!"

You run to the river, and jump back, in horror. "Blood! The whole river's full of blood!"

"Yes, it's—" No one waits to hear the general.

"Let's get out of here!" Chris starts running toward the mountains, but you stop him.

"Don't go there! LOOK!" The mountain no longer looks like a mountain, but like a great dragon. The beast opens his mouth and three froglike evil spirits come out. The devils start directing the armies amassed at the foot of the dragon mountain.

"Listen to me! This is—" A great peal of thunder drowns out K's words.

Lightning flashes, thunder rolls, the mountain shakes, and buildings around you start to crumble. Huge hailstones, some of them weighing a hundred pounds, fall from the sky.

"It's Armageddon!" the general yells above the noise of the storm. "I forgot until too late that it was to be fought at Megiddo. This is . . ."

Turn to page 147.

You catch the next double-decker bus that comes by and scramble up the curved stairs to the top, where you enjoy your ride through London. You get off at the stop marked Westminster and stand, openmouthed, looking up at the 350-foot-high clock tower.

"It looks like it was built out of gold lace," your sister says, and for once you don't think she's stupid.

"Yes, it does, now that it's been cleaned. It used to be almost black." Heather leads the way to an entrance guarded by a bobby in his high, rounded police hat. Then she stops suddenly. "Oh, I forgot. There have been so many bombing threats that the Houses of Parliament are closed to the public. I'm afraid I brought you down here all for nothing."

"Oh, that's okay. It was a fun bus ride," you say.

As soon as he hears your voice, the bobby moves towards you.

"We're going," you say quickly, holding up your hand.

But he speaks to Heather. "These are two American children, just arrived today?"

Heather nods, and to your great surprise he mentions your name.

"Won't you please come in? There is someone here to see you."

Turn to page 66.

You fly AL the small distance across one corner of the Plain of Esdrealon to the Megiddo Pass, the way through the mountains on the main road to Jerusalem.

Brother Hugh greets you at the gate of the massive stone fortification occupied by the Knights Templar. It strikes you as strange that this man—and all the others you meet—are dressed as knights, but their manner is that of monks.

"Yes, we are knights who fight fearlessly," Brother Hugh tells you, "but we are also monks who take holy vows."

"Pilgrims to the Holy Land often arrive ill and exhausted from their journey. Others are beset by brigands on the road to Jerusalem. We care for the sick, the elderly, the poor, and the hungry, and aid and protect travelers."

You are given rooms in the castle and invited to join the monks at their prayers and then at dinner, which is nourishing but very plain.

After dinner there are more prayers. The service is almost over when the jangle of a bell sounds throughout the castle, telling the Templars that a band of pilgrims has arrived.

"We seek refuge and protection," they say. "Saladin's men are on the march. They could be here tomorrow—we must get to Jerusalem."

Choices: You stay at Faba to defend the castle (turn to page 111).

You go to protect the pilgrims (turn to page 92).

Chris backs down with you. You scrape your hands on the rough stone, and blood mixes with the sweat to make your grip even slicker. You feel yourself slipping and grab desperately.

But there's nothing to grab onto.

THE END

110

"Hold onto me, Chris!" you yell, leaning out over the open pit.

Chris holds your hand, but the rain makes it slick. As you lean forward, your hand slips from Chris's grasp, and you pitch headfirst into the murky hole.

At least the mud makes a soft landing.

"You okay?" Chris yells.

"Yeah, fine. I've found something. A sort of urn. Can you reach it?"

You hold the large clay object up to Chris.

He lies down in the mud, but can't quite reach you. "Wait. I'll get the general," he yells.

You hope he hurries. It's dark and cold in the wet pit, and you're all alone.

But not for long. Chris lies down in the mud again, and with General K holding his ankles, he's able to lean into the pit and take the urn from you. Then he leans down again and pulls you out. The three of you sit in the mud looking at the red clay jug. It's about three feet high and sealed tightly. You shake it, and something rattles softly inside.

Choices: You break the pot (turn to page 41).
You think you should take it to an expert (turn to page 148).

Before it is light the next morning, the pilgrims leave to make their way through the dangerous Megiddo Pass. After seeing them off, you go with Brother Hugh and the other warrior-monks to Lauds, the five o'clock prayers which end at dawn.

The last echoes of the monks' chants have barely faded from the stone chapel when another kind of sound shreds the air—a high-pitched shriek which tears across the desert above the pounding of horses' hooves. A moment later a hail of arrows falls on the courtyard, announcing the arrival of Saladin's savage warriors.

The clash of arms resounds from every side of the massive fort as the Saracens storm the walls. The Templars battle valiantly. Every man is true to his vow not to flee in battle, but to fight to the death against the infidels.

You never see what happens to Chris or General K, but as a stab of fiery, searing pain fills your chest you hear Brother Hugh cry, "A fearful massacre, oh, Lord God, forgive them, and receive your servants this day into your presence."

THE END

You eat a quick breakfast in the officers' mess and stay close to General K. It's great to be with someone who knows his way around so well. He orders horses for all of you and pulls Elizabeth up in the saddle behind him so you can ride out to watch the battle.

You see the cloud of dust approach before you see the cavalry divisions. Then you as much feel the horses thundering over the ground as hear them. The charge sweeps into the valley and there is only scattered gunfire.

"Took 'em by surprise!" General K yells.
"Caught the Turks napping!

Half a league, half a league,
Half a league onward,
All in the valley of Death
Rode the six hundred.
'Forward, the Light Brigade!
Charge for the guns!' he said:
Into the valley of Death
Rode the six hundred."

You move your finger in a circle at your
forehead and point at K, but Chris shakes his
head. "It's a poem—'The Charge of the Light
Brigade.' We read it in school."

"Awful mess that was," K says, "but this
makes up for it. You've seen an historic victory,
my friends—the last great cavalry charge in the
annals of war.

"Allenby will push on to Damascus. I shall
follow him."

You look at Chris, who says, "I checked out
that map in headquarters. Noticed something
interesting!"

Choices: You persuade Chris to follow Allenby
with General K (turn to page 65).
You go with Chris (turn to page 116).

King Philip is not a fighter, but he is a good strategist, so General Kempthorne is excited about sailing home with him. "That man is only twenty-five and blind in one eye, but he is the shrewdest, most calculating spinner of plots I've ever met. This is a perfect opportunity—we'll have the whole voyage across the Mediterranean Sea to discuss battle plans. I couldn't have hoped for the mission to turn out better!"

King Philip says he's done his duty as a Christian by helping at the seige of Acre and claims his frail health is breaking down in the heat, but you think he's leaving because he's jealous of Richard's fame.

The English are angered by Philip's departure, calling it a cowardly desertion. Most of France's best knights stay with Richard. You're unhappy about leaving like this. When a royal messenger hurries past, you decide to follow him to Richard's tent.

You arrive just in time to hear Richard thunder, "Bring me someone who will sail to England immediately! Someone loyal!"

You hesitantly step inside the tent and bow. "I sail with the tide, Your Majesty."

"I have received word of my brother, Prince John's, treachery. He thinks to take over my throne while I'm out of the country. He must be stopped!"

"Yes, sir, Your Majesty!"

You "set sail" in AL at once.

Turn to page 12.

AL has barely settled into the desert sands of the Holy Land when General K yanks the door open and strides over to the British Army Headquarters—he doesn't even need a costume to blend in.

You follow along a little more slowly, and by the time you get there the officers are already discussing strategy.

"Surprise and capture of water supplies will be your prime objectives, I expect," K says.

Allenby is a tall, big-boned man. His dark moustache and bald head add emphasis to his commanding manner as he points at a map. "We'll mass the bulk of our forces in the coastal plain and cross the Samarian ridge by Mount Carmel above the Bay of Acre. Then we'll sweep down into the plain of Esdraelon and pass through the Valley of Jezreel—throwing a net around the Turkish armies."

"Jolly good," K says. "That should give you a superiority of four to one in cavalry."

"Quite so. We attack at 4:30 in the morning."

When you hear that, you and Chris take Elizabeth off to get some sleep. But the troops are up before three, and so is Elizabeth.

"Take me for a walk," she begs.

Choices: You say no; you want to stay to watch the battle (turn to page 112).

You do as she asks (turn to page 44).

Chris points across the valley. "That's Endor. Ring any bells?"

You shake your head. "Should it?"

"Famous witch lived there—the Witch of Endor. King Saul visited her."

"You're kidding. Witches aren't real."

Chris shrugs. "This one's in the Bible."

AL's chronograph rolls back to the time of King Saul, and you all change into Bible costumes.

"I'm scared of witches," Elizabeth says.

"Don't be a baby!" you yell at her, so Chris won't guess that you're a little worried, too.

At first you think everyone in the town is asleep, but then you spot three shadowy figures ahead of you. They lead you to a tent on the edge of the village, and you peek in.

"I'll pay you to call up the spirit of the one I wish to speak to," the tallest of the robed figures says.

The old woman in the doorway jumps back. "It's a trap! King Saul has ordered all witches put to death!"

"Call up the spirit of the prophet Samuel and nothing will happen to you," he orders.

The witch kneels before a fire in the center of the room and peers into the smoke. "Samuel . . . Samuel . . . Samuel . . ." Then she shrieks and falls back.

Turn to page 145.

You run to your friends, calling, "Hey, those guys tried to poison me!"

"What?" Chris yells.

"Well, maybe." You calm down a little. "They wanted me to eat fruit from Saladin—it *could* have been poisoned."

The general laughs at you. "Indeed, it could have been—but it wasn't. Saladin is—was—a highly civilized man. When Saladin's archers shot Richard's horse from under him, the sultan sent Richard two new horses—or rather, will send, after it happens—but then it all happened about 800 years ago—time travel is very confusing."

"Have you had enough, sir?" Chris asks. "Shall we go home?"

General K nods.

You don't think getting back to London such a bad idea yourself. But it doesn't turn out to be a very practical one.

Chris hits the cartograph and groans, "I knew it was tricky, but I really thought it'd work."

"Do you mean to say we can't move?" K asks.

"Only in time, not in space." Chris shakes his head. "Well, want to see how Richard does next year?"

"No. Into the future—our future, not Richard's!" General Kempthorne says.

Choices: You shake your head at Chris. "No, Richard's future," you say (turn to page 64).
You nod your agreement to Chris (turn to page 106).

"No sense in going all that way on a horse—or worse yet, walking—when we've got AL," you tell Heather and Elizabeth. You set the dials to arrive in Canterbury just as Chaucer's pilgrims get there two weeks later. You enter the cathedral with them and walk up the long chancel under the forest of arches. You move slowly, reverently, up the flight of stone steps leading to Thomas à Becket's tomb. Already grooves are being worn in the stone from the feet of hundreds of pilgrims.

With the others, you kneel before the shrine. It is covered with great plates of gold encrusted with diamonds, rubies, and emeralds. A priest points out various jewels, explaining which king or prince gave each one. "This jewel is the *Regale de France,* which King Louis VII offered for the safe deliverance of his son from illness."

Many around you are praying for similar miracles.

The priest finishes his lecture and presents each of you with a pilgrim's badge—a pewter figure of Thomas surrounded with ornate filigree in the shape of the cathedral's gothic arches. You hold yours in your hand and look at it. This is something you will keep always, to remind you of Thomas's courage and sacrifice and of the pilgrims' faith and devotion.

THE END

Turning your head so you don't have to look at the red stains on the sand, you take a small bag of gold from a fallen Turkish soldier. You move to the next body and pull several jewel-encrusted rings off his fingers. You are doing well collecting loot when Chris runs up.

"AL's gone!"

"Gone? Gone where?"

"Into a million zillion pieces—smashed into the sand. He was parked in the way of the cavalry charge."

You sit down in the sand to think, just missing a pool of blood on one side and a broken sword on the other. "You mean we're stuck here? In the middle of all these bodies? What about my sister and Heather? What am I gonna do about them?" Your voice gets more worried with each question.

You think about praying and glance up at the sky. As you do, a whole new idea comes to you—you see one of the anchored, hot air balloons Napoleon uses for observation.

"Get the others and meet me there!" you shout, pointing. You start running.

By the time Chris has collected the others, you've pulled the balloon down and are climbing into the gondola basket. General K takes the sword from a fallen Turk and slashes the anchor rope. You float away to safety.

Almost.

"Look out! We're gonna hit the top of Mt. Tabor!" Chris yells.

You all start tossing out sandbags. The bal-

loon lifts a few feet higher. It isn't enough. The
mountaintop looms as Elizabeth sobs.

You know what you have to do. Emptying the
gold and jewels from your pockets, you lift
enough to clear the mountain.

THE END

"Sorry, I've got thirty pilgrims here ahead of you—not to mention Master Geoffrey Chaucer, who works at the court of King Henry IV himself. No rooms left." The innkeeper shakes his head at you.

"Well," you say with a shrug, "guess we can sleep in AL."

In all the adventures you've had in AL, sleeping in him is a new one. He wasn't exactly designed for the purpose, but you're so sleepy it seems simpler just to put your head down on the console and drift off than to fly to another time or place looking for a motel.

Elizabeth lays her head in Heather's lap, and that's the last you remember until noises outside wake you in the morning.

"Wow, I feel as though I've slept for about 600 years!" you say. You try to stretch in the cramped quarters. "Let's go on our pilgrimage!"

You jump out of AL and see a monk in his heavy brown robe and rope sandals cross the courtyard, his hands folded. He must be the monk in Chaucer's party. You run to catch up with him as he turns the corner to the stables.

You round the corner just in time to see the monk gather his robes and ride off—in a sleek silver Porsche.

You turn back to Heather and Elizabeth. "I, uh, guess I bumped something in my sleep. Now we'll have to start all over."

THE END

Elizabeth begins to whimper. You hold her hand while backing as far into a dark corner as you can. The light from the case glints off Blood's long hair and bulbous nose, making him look more horrible than ever.

With an ear-splitting crash, the battle-ax splinters the glass case. You bend over Elizabeth, protecting her from flying shards of glass with your body. You feel something sharp rip through your shirt and a warm trickle run down your spine. You bite your lip to keep from crying out. There's no sense in scaring your sister worse than she already is.

Suddenly Colonel Blood's laughter turns to angry curses as he discovers that the door he slammed shut is locked. He starts slashing at it with the battle-ax.

The door starts to break, but the ancient weapon gives out first and the axe handle breaks. Blood picks up the golden royal sceptre with the Star of Africa in the end and aims it at the door.

"No!" you shout, without thinking. "It'll break!" The last thing you remember is seeing the Star of Africa hurtling toward your head.

THE END

As you walk, you listen to the men around you talk.

"Eh, blimey, we're not above twelve miles from Jerusalem."

"Can't be. I don't see no signs of a city."

"There's mountains between here and there, blockhead. But Jerusalem's there, all right and tight."

"I believe ya. A few more days will see us in the Holy City, and that will be the end of those infidel Turks thinkin' they can rule God's own country."

The men's encouraging words raise your spirits, and you run ahead to where Richard is talking with some of his most powerful knights. A bit of listening to them, and you wish you'd stayed behind.

"If we try to besiege Jerusalem, we'll starve first—all our supplies come from the coast."

"That's right, and those miserable Saracens destroy most of our convoys."

"It is time to sue for peace." Richard's voice holds immense sadness. "I will send a messenger—" he looks around and sees you. "You there! I want you to go to Saladin. I will meet him to discuss the terms of treaty. But not in Jerusalem—I will not look on the city I cannot capture."

Richard has ordered; you have no choice. Turn to page 77.

"You know, if we climb that hill, we can see a lot of these places," General K looks from the map to the land around him. Since the rain has stopped and a feeble sun is trying to shine, his suggestion doesn't sound too bad.

You climb the hill at the back of the ancient city of Megiddo, which guards the pass through the mountains and looks out across the great Plain of Esdraelon stretching like a smooth, green sea to the distant hills. The shadows of clouds pass over, and you think of the ghosts of the old armies K is talking about.

"There are over twenty battlefields down there. For hundreds of years the plain was hardly ever without the thunder of chariot wheels and the clash of weapons." He points to the right. "That's Mount Carmel over there—where Elijah drew down fire from heaven against the priests of Baal. And there—" he points at Megiddo below you— "King Solomon built one of his cities of chariots with stables for 110 horses." General Kempthorne sighs and places his hand over his heart, "I say, doesn't that move you with the pride, the pomp, the pageantry of history."

"Uh, yeah, sure," you say.

"Uh-huh, but I'm hungry," Chris adds.

The general looks disgusted, but he says, "Right-o. Since your flying machine is kaput, I shall contact Her Majesty's Royal Air Force for transport to London."

THE END

You go to the White Tower, with its fifteen-foot-thick walls. "Wow! What a fortress!"

Then you go into the medieval armor gallery and again you say, "Wow!" In front of you is a mounted knight—both man and horse in full plate armor.

You walk back in time through the rooms filled with cases of arms and armor: fancy tournament armor of the 16th century, mail-and-plate armor worn by the Black Prince in the 14th century, chain mail with a surcoat over it like that the Crusaders wore in the 12th century.

You imagine riding on a crusade beside Richard the Lionheart, with banners flying beneath the burning desert sun to rescue the Holy Land from the infidel turks . . . Suddenly you realize that somebody is calling your name.

"Chris! What are you doing here?"

"Looking for you. Figured you'd come to see this first."

"Yeah, but how? and why?"

"Professor Q sent me. The Pentagon called. Some bigwig NATO general wants to go back in history to study the strategy of famous battles. So here I am. I mean, you don't say no to the U.S. Army and NATO."

"Yeah. Right. But how'd you get here?"

"In AL, of course."

"AL? Since when does his cartograph include Europe?"

"New computer chip. But I should warn you— it's not working exactly right. The general's call came so soon that we didn't get a chance to test it. It should be okay, though."

Choices: You say, "I'm not going anywhere till it's tested!" (turn to page 72).

You say, "Well, get this general and let's go" (turn to page 60).

The general taps the bill of his hat with his baton. "A Number 9 bus will take you to Grosvenor Square. Inquire of the NATO attache. You will find my credentials quite in order."

At Grosvenor Square you can't believe your eyes. "Are you *sure* this is the *American* Embassy?" you ask the guard. The question is dumb, since he's an American marine, but the square, block-long, gray cement building is incredibly ugly. "It looks a lot more like something the Russians would design," you say.

Still shaking your head, you are led down a corridor past row after row of office doors. You finally come to one where you are told to wait. And wait. And wait.

"Sorry you had to wait so long," says a thin-faced young man in a dark suit and thick glasses. He crosses the room from an inner door. "I'm Michaels. What can I help you with?"

You tell him you need information on General Kempthorne, hoping he won't ask you for a security pass or something. Without another word, he leads you into his office. You wait again while he pokes at a computer, looks up a file, and makes a phone call. You get nervous when he presses a button, and two marines march into the office.

Choices: You run (turn to page 30).
          You wait (turn to page 95).

You hold the peach in your hand, rosy and golden. Drops of melted snow trickle into your palm. You don't see any pricks on the skin, but then, Saladin wouldn't be that obvious, would he?

Everyone in the tent, including King Richard, is looking at you. You close your eyes and, trying not to think about a piercing, cramping stomachache or a burning, closing throat, you take a bite.

After holding the fruit in your mouth for a moment you force yourself to swallow. The peach is the sweetest, juiciest fruit you've ever tasted. You feel great.

The physician directs Richard's men to cool his drink with the snow and offers the king a piece of fruit. You are the only person besides Richard who gets to taste the delicacy.

The cool refreshment eases the King, and he begins discussing battle strategy with his knights. In order to breach the walls of Acre, the tower must be scaled and more war machines built.

Action at last!

Choices: You want to scale the tower (turn to page 20).

You want to help build machines (turn to page 40).

"This can *really* take us back in time—to *anything* we want to see?" Heather asks, looking around inside AL.

"Sure," you say. "Pick something."

Heather closes the door and helps Elizabeth with her seat belt. "All right. How about the Tabard Inn across the river from London? April of 1387."

You set the dials and gauges. "Why?"

"Well, after being at Canterbury, I thought it would be fun to meet Chaucer and the people he wrote about in the *The Canterbury Tales.*

AL settles down, and you arrive at the inn just as a band of dusty, weary travelers cross the London Bridge and enter the courtyard. All is abustle as the ostler takes the horses, a knight and lady demand rooms and food, a monk and prioress ask for a place to wash, and a lawyer requires a fire be laid.

In the middle of all the confusion is a little man with a pointed white beard, jotting notes on a sheet of parchment. "There he is," Heather points. "That's Chaucer—the father of English literature, the first great poet in our language."

You think that sounds kind of boring, until he looks up and smiles at you. A man with such a humorous smile just might be fun to know.

Then a yawn about splits your face.

Choices: You want to stay up and meet Chaucer (turn to page 136).
You say, "I want to go to bed" (turn to page 122).

"Great! Let's go on the third Crusade with King Richard!"

On the way to AL, you and Chris stop at the Tower gift shop and buy imitation suits of chain mail. You don't want to look as though you came from outer space, in your jeans and sneakers. The general says his uniform is proper anyplace, anytime.

In AL, Chris's friend General K directs you to set the cartograph for the ancient city of Acre, a seaport near the Plain of Esdraelon. Chris hesitates over the chronograph.

"1191," the general says.

The city of Acre is a mosaic of history. You stand on the side on Mount Turon and see the slender minaret of a Turkish mosque, Arabian arches, and massive Crusader fortifications surrounded with moats, looking over the city wall. But you stay outside, because Acre is a city under siege. And the beseiging Crusaders are themselves besieged by the Turks.

Food is scarce. You see a man wearing the Crusader cross kill his horse for food. Another eats grass, and another chews on bare bones.

The general looks around and shakes his head. "King Richard hasn't arrived. Perhaps we should seek refuge with the knights Templar at the castle of Faba."

Choices: You join the Templars (turn to page 108).
You await Richard's arrival (turn to page 6).

You get to the Visitors' Center and start looking at the displays about Robin Hood when you hear someone running. Before you can turn around, you feel a hand on your shoulder.

"I yelled and yelled. Why didn't you stop?"

The voice is angry, but you recognize it. "Chris! What are you doing here?"

"We've got a mission with AL—we're supposed to take General Kempthorne into history to study battle strategy."

"General *who*?" you say.

Just then a man in an English army uniform walks up—with Elizabeth holding his hand. He lets go of her hand to shake yours. "This young lady asked me to escort her here while her nanny takes a tea break."

"Well, I can understand Heather needing a break from Elizapest," you say. "Shall we take her with us?"

Elizabeth thinks AL is another fair ride and is all excited.

"Quiet!" you yell at her, so you can hear General K's instructions.

"The Megiddo Valley, September 18, 1918, to see General Sir Edmund Allenby lead one of the historic battles of World War I. I've just been visiting with his ancestors in Nottingham. This was his home, you know."

No, you didn't know but you set the dials anyway.

Turn to page 115.

In your worry over your sister it seems like you're a long time thrashing through the woods. Finally you come to a clearing and find Robin's men.

There, in the middle of them, is Elizabeth, crunching on an apple and telling Little John, who is nearly seven feet tall, all about her adventure.

"But how did you make them let go of you?" he asks.

"I said I had to—" she whispers in his ear, and Little John bursts out laughing.

"Well done, lass. But how did you know which way to run?"

"I heard laughing. Everyone knows Robin Hood's men were merry—are merry, I mean."

They all laugh at this. Elizabeth sees you and comes to give you a hug.

And with your sister safe, you feel merry, too.

THE END

Doron pulls you up. Chris makes it on his own. "Now we do *Shizumi aruki*—low-position walking—along top of wall to stairs. Like this. Watch." Doron squats down to half his height and moves forward, swinging his arms for balance. You follow awkwardly to a narrow, winding staircase. Doron is the first into the courtyard, but you never leave the shelter of the stairway.

The master has walked straight into John's guards. It's all your fault for not really telling him what the situation was. You hold your breath to see what he'll do.

Doron is held at sword point by two of John's men. Feet wide apart, knees bent, Doron visibly relaxes, holding his sheathed sword in a non-threatening position in front of him.

The watchmen bark orders and thrust their swords at Doron. He starts to obey and the soldiers drop their guard. Then Doron whirls, throwing blinding powder at one man and slashing the other.

The guards defeated, the Ninja lunges toward the stairs.

"Run!" you yell at Chris. "He knows we tricked him. We're next!"

THE END

In the main room of the inn, before a roaring fire, long tables are set with wooden trenchers, which they use for plates. The travelers take places at the tables, and the cooks bring in the food: fish, fowl, and meats cooked in garlic, onions, mustard, vinegar, and spices; bacon and pea soup; puddings and pastries; and tankards of drinks.

After you have all eaten, Chaucer stands on a bench by the fireplace and claps his hands for attention. "Let us begin our program of amusements. For those who have just joined us," he says, looking at your party, "we have agreed, for our mutual entertainment, to tell tales as we travel. Each pilgrim is to tell two tales on the journey to Canterbury, and two on the return trip."

He pauses to take a drink from his pewter tankard. "Since this is your first night with us, I propose that you be our first storyteller."

Everyone looks at you.

Choices: You dive for the door, dragging Heather and Elizabeth with you, and say, "I'll meet you at Canterbury" (turn to page 119).

You walk very slowly to the front of the room to give yourself time to think (turn to page 67).

You hang around in the pouring rain for a long time, but finally Chris and a tall, military fellow show up. Chris is amazed to see you, especially since he looked all over London for you. He finally gave up and came on down here for some sight-seeing with General Kempthorne. Chris introduces his companion, who is on assignment from NATO to study battle strategies from history.

"We went to Dover Beach and rode the hovercraft across the English Channel to France. You know—it's like a boat, only it floats *above* the water! And now General K is all into French history and wants to go see Napoleon in action. Want to go along?"

"All of us?" You point to Elizabeth and Heather.

"Sure. AL won't mind if we squeeze a bit."

The squeeze is more than a bit, but you manage to close the door. "Where to?"

"The plain of Esdraelon in the Holy Land. April, 1799. I want to see Napoleon in battle before he becomes emperor."

Turn to page 139.

You think you've made enough choices for one day. But as soon as you get off the train in Nottingham, Heather asks, "Do you want to go to the castle in the center of town or out in the country to Sherwood Forest?"

You hesitate. "What's to see?"

"The castle is now a museum with armor and dungeons and lots of stuff," Heather says. "In the forest is the Major Oak where Robin Hood's men hid from the sheriff and Shambles Oak where Robin Hood hung his venison—and farther on, Robin Hood's grave."

Choices: You want to climb the high, rocky hill to the castle (turn to pge 84).

You decide to take a bus through the green countryside to Sherwood forest (turn to page 99).

You see him sooner than you expect. You've no more than stepped out of AL than a dark, handsome man in a three-corner hat, his right hand thrust into his waistcoat, canters up to a batallion of calvary troops.

"Men!" he cries. "Tomorrow we meet the Turks. It shall be a glorious victory for France!" The men cheer. "But to ensure that the glory is ours, I need a small party of volunteers to slip into the enemy camp tonight."

That sounds exciting. You look at your companions.

Choices: You want to spy for Napoleon (turn to page 15).
You'd rather stay with the cavalry (turn to page 56).

It's easy to slip in with the hunting party servants. You and Chris each pick up an end of a pole with a deer's legs tied to it and carry it over your shoulders all the way up to Nottingham Castle. Your shoulders ache like you can't believe by the time you get there

"Now let's get out of here," you say to Chris.

You start toward the door, but the way is blocked by the chief steward, a giant of a man wielding two large knives. He thrusts them at you. "Skin it!" he commands in a voice that clearly says he'll skin you if you don't obey.

The knife is clumsy and the deer hide tough, but it's kind of fun at first. Then you start getting blisters on your hand. The knife slips, and you cut your finger. You wipe the sweat off your forehead and smear yourself with blood—yours and the deer's.

"That's it!" You toss your knife down. "Let's go find K and get out of here. I've had it!"

Chris, who looks even worse than you do, agrees. You turn toward the door just in time to see the chief steward enter. "The Duke of Kempthorne sends his regards. He is taking the Earl of Norfolk on a journey to the castle NATO. You are to continue in Prince John's service until he returns."

You sit down in a pool of blood on the stone floor. "Can General K fly AL?" you ask.

"I hope so," Chris says.

"I hope he can fly enough to get back for us."

THE END

"No! Don't let her die before she wakes, God!" you yell.

As if in answer, there is a knock at the door and a turbaned servant enters with a tray—fruit juice, cheese, and biscuits. You thank him, and then take another look at the food. "Gross! She can't eat this—it's rotten!"

Chris looks at the cheese covered with little blue, fuzzy dots and the likewise moldy biscuits. "Choke 'em down her if you have to."

"What! She's already sick—you want to kill her with rotten food?"

"Penicilin." Chris points to the mold. "That's what it's made from."

You're sure she'll throw it all up, and you'll have to clean up the mess, but miraculously she doesn't. And in a few hours she's better.

"Told you I got an A in science," Chris says.

You think for a minute. "People are sick all over town. Wonder how much of that moldy cheese they've got?"

Chris nods. "It's worth a try."

A week later the epidemic is over. You realize you might have done as much to help win World War I as if you'd charged with the cavalry. Matter of fact, you think you might consider going to medical school someday.

THE END

"You're crazy! We'll never get over that wall."
Chris stands with head back, looking almost
straight up.

"We might, I have an idea. Before I met you I
saw some guys from a Ninjutsu school—"

"Ninjas! Around here?" Chris almost yells.

"Shh. Edwinstowe, their badges said. Isn't
that the next village?"

"You think one would come with us in AL?"

"Maybe. If we explain that it's a really important—er—rescue operation. You got any better
ideas?"

Chris doesn't, so it's lucky that the Ninja
master is willing to come with you—and to
supply you with tabi boots for wall climbing.
You don't really lie to him; you just don't bother
telling him about the time-travel bit. After all, the
castle wall hasn't changed all that much, so
what difference does it make? And he might
refuse if he knew the whole story.

Clad in his black uniform, his sword at this side, Doron explains, *"Ishigaki* means stonewall. The Ninja hugs the rocks closely, using every crack and crevice for hand and footholds. Tabi boots will help. I show you. You two follow."

Clinging to the wall, his hood covering his face, Doron disappears into the shadows.

Little John was right about the rough stones making handles, and the tabi boots help a lot. About halfway up you start sweating. No good—you don't need slick hands.

"I can't move," you say. You hope you don't sound as scared as you feel.

"Here." Doron reaches his scabbard down to you. "I pull you up."

Choices: **You grab hold of the scabbard (turn to page 135).**

You try backing down—slowly (turn to page 109).

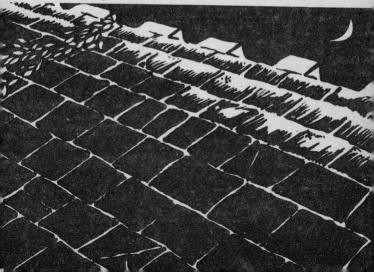

Elizabeth is sobbing. "Those men were so mean. Why did they do that?"

"Thomas and the king had been fighting for years—all about the freedom of the church versus royal power," Heather explains. "When he became king, Henry appointed his best friend as archbishop so he could tell him what to do—but Thomas said God was above the king."

"Who was the king?" you ask.

"Henry II. His sons were Richard the Lionheart and Prince John."

You hug Elizabeth. "Shh, Lizard, don't cry. Pretend you saw it on TV—it's all over now."

But there is something you're worrying about. "Heather, all that stuff Thomas said about the Christian way being not to fight—in the Bible, God told people to go to war."

Heather nods. "That's a tough one, isn't it? Sometimes we have to fight to defend God-given freedoms. If failing to fight would mean people could no longer worship freely, then *refusing* to fight would be nonchristian."

The monks are chanting a descant for the dead and preparing Thomas's body for burial. Elizabeth is still sobbing. You feel bad that the adventure you planned turned out so rotten.

"Hey, I know!" you say. "Let's go back to AL. I remember seeing an ice-cream parlor near the cathedral—it had a lighted fountain bubbling lemonade and everything."

Elizabeth looks up. "Strawberry ice cream?"

THE END

"*You* are Saul!" the witch cries. "The spirit told me!"

But Saul ignores her. Samuel is speaking from the smoke. "Saul, Saul, because you disobeyed God, the Lord will deliver Israel into the hands of her enemies. Tomorrow you and your sons will be dead."

King Saul falls on the floor in a faint.

"Pretty impressive, huh?" Chris says. "Let's ask her something."

Choices: You speak to the witch (turn to page 23).
You say, "No, let's get back to Allenby" (turn to page 46).

You hurry Heather and Elizabeth into AL. "Lizard's had enough excitement for one day," you say to Heather, and for once Elizabeth is too tired to argue. "Why don't you take her back to London? I want to stick around here and see my friend. I can find my way back to the hotel later."

Heather starts to object, but then Elizabeth drifts off to sleep on her lap, so she agrees.

When you get back to your own time in Canterbury, the rain still hasn't let up. Heather goes to the train station, carrying Elizabeth in one arm and an umbrella in the other. At least you can stay dry waiting inside AL.

You grin to yourself. Chris is going to be surprised when he opens the door and sees you.

But you get the surprise. The door jerks open and you are staring down the barrel of a heavy, black revolver.

"What are you doing here?" a man in uniform demands.

"Don't shoot, General K! That's my friend—the one we've been looking for."

You're relieved to hear Chris's voice behind the man.

The general puts his gun away, and you relax as Chris explains that General Kempthorne is a NATO officer who wants to travel in AL to study battles of the past.

"Would you like to see Richard the Lionheart, sir?" you ask, still shaking a bit inside.

General K says he certainly would.

Turn to page 132.

"I think there's a university at Haifa," General K says. "They'll have an archaeology department that'll know what to do with this."

"Haifa?" you ask, "Where's that?"

"Back near Acre."

"Back to Acre! After we've walked all this way?"

"Well," Chris says, "AL can get us to modern times. Maybe it won't be raining then."

"Yeah!" you say, "Maybe we can hitchhike!"

That's exactly what you do. A theatre group touring in a bus thinks your Crusades outfits are great, even though they can't figure out how you got them so muddy.

"Part of the costume," you tell them. "We're in a pageant that's reenacting the part of the third Crusade where Richard's troops get stuck in the mud."

"Sounds great! Wish we could see you, but

we've got a performance tonight." They let you off at the university.

The head of the archaeology department is thrilled with your discovery. "A find comparable to the Dead Sea Scrolls! Can you show me the location?"

You start to say sure, and then remember that you found the urn 800 years ago. "Well, I don't know. . . ."

Then he talks about rewards. "There is very little money in archaeology, but perhaps some kind of national grant—"

"That won't be necessary," you say quickly, "but do you have a good computer department here?"

"Of course, most advanced."

"That's great, because we need highly special-ized chip for our computer. That would mean more to us than any prize."

THE END

The mighty war machine creaks with the weight of fifty knights in armor. You climb the narrow stairway between the iron and bronze levels, trying not to think of the army you must face on the other side of the wall. Too late you realize you aren't even armed.

Just as you come out on the top level, something sails through the air, barely missing your head. A clay pot crashes against the stone rampart, and a clear liquid spills out and runs down the wall. You don't like the smell of alcohol, but the confident crusaders around you laugh. "What's all this, then—throwing their waterpots at us?"

You jump onto the wall of the city with Chris at your heels, when a flaming arrow lands among the pieces of the broken pot. Immediately a wall of flame engulfs the tower.

The last thing you hear is the general's agonized yell, "Greek fire!"

THE END

YOU'RE IN COMMAND!

Your dad is taking the whole family along on a business trip to England . . . but when you meet up with General Kempthorne of NATO, you know you won't be just another tourist in the crowd. You might

   . . . travel back to Sherwood Forest in search of Robin Hood.

   . . . join the Crusades with Richard the Lionheart.

   . . . stop a jewel heist in the Tower of London.

MAKING CHOICES BOOKS let you create your own stories with the choices you make, page by page. It's great practice in Christian decision making. But, unlike real life, if you don't like the way things are turning out in your story, you can go back and start over! Over thirty possible endings!

A FAVORITE SERIES OF KIDS EVERYWHERE!
"It's an adventure to read these books because you make the choices. They are exciting books."
                 Zac Hansel, 12
                 San Dimas, California

"I like choosing things that if I really did them I could get in a heap of trouble."
                 Jeff Sommer,
                 Owosso, Mich

IL 9-14

50344 A4800

ISBN 1-55513-034-8

Chariot Books
DAVID C. COOK PUBLISHING CO.